Visits to Issaquah

By

Nathan Kositsky

Visits to Issaquah

Requests for permission to make copies of any part of the work should be mailed to:
Permission Department
Tundra Girl Press
Box 1021
Snoqualmie, WA 98065

ISBN 978-0-9849837-0-4

Kindle Edition ISBN 978-0-9849837-1-1

Book and cover design: Magdalena Bassett
Cover photo: DJ Bassett, www.bassettstudio.com

Visits to Issaquah

I

One Memory

LEAVE SAN DIEGO WITH ONE MEMORY. THE TIRE SPINS OFF MY Avanti as I speed down Interstate 805. The car dips. The steering wheel pulls in my hand west toward Chula Vista and I don't know what happened. Not yet I don't. But the wheel nut, the one Marvin the Mobile Mechanic screwed on wrong, has just shot sideways like a bullet, causing the tire, the wheel, the whole thing, to spin off and bounce beside the car.

I've been following a Subaru Forester, trying to read its bumper sticker *Don't Believe Everything You Think*. Now the Subaru is a dot down the highway and the tire is ahead of me picking up speed. It bounces down an off-ramp. I follow it scraping flames. Now it becomes clear. That's *my* tire ahead of me. It bounces up and down in slow motion like my years here in San Diego. Up and down. Up and down. It bounces up to the waist of a person, now up to the height of a person.

Leave San Diego with that memory. Not because this is my last day here. Not because this is the place that blew the full note of what it means for me to be a human being on Earth. But because just when a person finally has a chance to squeeze through a tiny closing opening, this is how a place you're trying to leave gets you. Leave San Diego with that memory.

The Avanti scrapes to a stop. The air is choking me. I smell fiberglass. The fiberglass is melting. I push on the door, push on the door. Now I'm on all fours in the off-ramp. My face lurches to breathe, to vomit. Warren conducting a soul-retrieval months from now, her face in profile turning up from the water fountain at Torrey Pines and Big Larry saying, "You'll *still* be on this porch telling me you're moving to Seattle."

"This yours?" a kid yells. He's up on his chain-link fence, holding up my wheel nut. It flashes in the sun.

I jerk-look him, and his head turns with mine down the off-ramp where the tire bounces once, twice and over the roof of a Honda then falls wobbling the way tires do.

"Did you *see* it?" I gasp, climbing his fence.

"You're some kind of lucky," he says.

We're both hanging at the top of his chain-link fence. The wheel nut enters my hand, warm, almost hot - a moment in time – and I drop from the fence and run toward the tire. Leave San Diego with that memory.

2

Seattle

SOME KIND OF LUCKY, WITH EMPHASIS ON THE SOME KIND OF, but someone is calling me Newt and it isn't my name. It's the next morning and I'm in Seattle. Behind me are a thousand last moments of escape, a plane ride, renting a vehicle, driving through the night to a dark, empty house – rattling, all rattling. So I guess that even leaving on good terms can't supress the larger truth. I must have slept on the floor in my sleeping bag. I'm near the window so the wind can blow fresh Northwest air over me. I remember now, that's what I called it when I closed the sleeping bag at my neck, fresh Northwest air.

"*Newt!*" the voice calls again, this time from downstairs. The doorbell is ringing. Do I have a doorbell? He weighs four hundred pounds with cologne adding another five pounds. He's sweating in the San Diego sun, taking inventory of the final moving boxes. He sticks a number on the last box and says, "Newt."

I say, "That's not my name."

"There's more here than was estimated," he says.

I can't get my eyes off his fat fingers.

"I have to go," Roxanne says, and a thing enters the air that this is it. Sometimes in a life the *one* is the one you don't realize. This is in the air. We're turning each other into holograms like test-memories, and like a test-memory she stands off the Avanti.

I'd met her through the Avanti. She'd been working in the courthouse where I'd taken action against Lou's Automotive for installing Ford parts in the steering column. It had revealed itself execute backwards, let go to turn, Your Honor, and the settlement had paid for months of dubious fix-its by Marvin the Mobile Mechanic, culminating in my near death three days from now. I follow Roxanne to her Ford Ranger. She buzzes down the window and places her brown arm on the sill. This is it.

"Newt," he says again and I pull back from the front door. He looks from me to his clipboard. "It's weighed high like I told you it might back in San Diego," he says and shoves the clipboard at me. "You'll need to sign," he says. "I don't haul free freight."

He is through the door, too, moving me back with his cologne.

"Do you hear the freeway?" I swallow. "Can you hear the freeway?"

"We don't set up beds," he replies.

His movers come through the door behind him.

"Just put that *there*. Kitchen goes in kitchen," he yells at them. Then he asks, "Is that right?"

"Kitchen goes in kitchen," I affirm.

From upstairs he calls, "Just tell us where to put things, Newt."

"Not Newt," I say, looking up at him through the breezeway.

"Don't know why I keep calling you that," he says out at the moving van.

"What do you think of the house compared to where I was?" I ask and I wave my hand across the exterior. "Nobody else may see both places. I just realized that," I say.

"Nice here nice there," he says. "I got a nice place, in Oregon."

"This place is bigger," I tell his back as it fills the front entrance again. Then I mutter, "Bigger," to myself and one of his movers says, "Don't worry about this guy. Enjoy your new place."

"But can you hear the freeway?" I ask and he stops listening to me except I don't know it. So I say, "The wind was blowing through the trees when I did the final walkthrough with the realtor. I wouldn't have bought this place if I'd known I could hear the freeway. I cut all ties in San Diego to give this place a chance. A chance is a lot to put on a place. My place in San Diego sold immediately and the transactions closed so quickly I didn't even know how to get here from SeaTac. I rented that Explorer. I was in an accident in San Diego... yesterday... a pretty bad accident... with my car."

Now I realize he isn't listening.

"My tire flew off," I say anyway. And I'm not done with his not listening. "Maybe you call it a wheel?" I ask. "I'm not sure if you call it a tire or a wheel. Actually, I think it's a tire that goes around a wheel. I worked with a guy who said he was always in the right place, but I didn't feel that way in San Diego. You know, not for a long time, in that part of the world. Is it always cold and overcast up here?" Then Newt's smell-arm appears over my neck with a clipboard appendage. A fat finger appears. "Initial here, Newt. Sign here, Newt," he says.

I initial. I sign and the signoff sheet moves away from me. Then the cologne moves away. I walk into the house. I open the kitchen window. I hear the moving van leave.

"I don't haul free freight." It lingers in the air like cologne.

Well, Newt, who does? Hauling freight comes at a cost. Anyway, reasons sound unhealthy rendered to a phrase. Best to keep your mouth shut. It's easier on strangers.

3

Julia

IT'S A COLD, GRAY AFTERNOON WITH SUN SPLOTCHES IN IT
as I walk away from the house and down the hill along the winding
rockery. Hanging over the rockery are huckleberries and blackberries.
Beyond the rockery are hemlock, fir and maple. Alders reach out bare
limbs. No memory superimposes. In San Diego every weed and brick
held a memory. It had become a place of ghosts, ghosts of things I'd
done to others and ghosts of things others had done to me. Here
bands of light could be bands of light. They stream through the entry
gate and splotch against the road. The overhanging blackberries dress
the alders like grapes. The smells are of fall, fresh and decaying, a
contradiction. The sky is low and lowering, and here comes Geodesic-
dome Joe, my fix-it neighbor in San Diego. He's offering me his
entire harvest of three blackberries from his twisted hand. His cuticles
are long and broken and touched with grease. I say to the Joe ghost,
"Here people contemplate ways to get rid of blackberries."

I stare at the blackberries and through them to the ghost of
Joe's hand. "Take three," he says and I eat two blackberries, body

of Christ, body of Christ, and my realtor drives up.

She's a tall, striking woman from Moscow. I've told her that her face should be on a stamp of Russia.

"Blackberries," I say, reaching out the last one to her.

My hand becomes the ghost of Joe's hand.

She smiles through bad teeth and her window comes down.

"Don't like," she says, and the reason is that she was a mail-order bride to a logger who fed her and her twin sister a precise diet of deer meat and potatoes. Now she's against any food she can see coming directly from nature. She's also against bad language because he fed her that too.

I eat the last blackberry from the ghost of Joe's hand and follow her car up to the house.

"The freeway," I say as she gets out of the car. "Can you hear the freeway?"

"What?" she asks.

We're inside the house now, looking at each other. She's sitting on one box and I'm sitting on another box. But she's sitting in a way that looked like she's standing. She's propped on an edge. Her long legs are stretched and spread. Her toes are pointed out. She's interested. She's provocative. She expects a man to be a man.

"The freeway," I repeat. "Can you hear the freeway?"

"It's an inversion layer," she says. "Freeway is very far away."

"What's an inversion layer? Thanks for making me feel like a foreigner," I say.

"Aren't we all foreigners?" she asks. "I too come from somewhere. I wish there was music. I *love* to dance."

"If I find my guitar," I say and she says, "I help you."

"No," I tell her, "I like looking at you where you are," and she says, "This is too professional. We know what we are doing." She repositions herself on the edge of the box. She says, "I wanted to be ballerina in Moscow. I wanted it so much but-"

"Yes?" I ask and she says, "But what you control are things that own you."

"Found it," I say.

She is dancing now and I'm playing my guitar and following her around the boxes. What a mover. When this guitar goes down she will. But for now she holds the pole in the living room and is shimmering up and down it, all six foot two of her, and what's a man to do when she loves to dance? I turn toward the picture window and the low sky ruptures and rain hits hard just like that.

"What was that song?" she asks.

"Something in the storm," I say.

The rain is hitting sideways now. The trees sway and scrape the tile roof.

I say, "Dancing spirits."

"*I* could be a tree," she says, moving in behind me.

"You could," I agree. "And there's a leak under the door. See it?"

"Yes," she says. "But now can't hear freeway. I want you to meet people. I have interesting people coming for my birthday party lecture at the university."

"I don't think that's a good idea," I say.

"Why?" she asks.

"Maybe I shouldn't say."

"You not like me? You not want see with me?"

"It's not that."

"Then what is reason?"

"I'm not used to explaining. I listen to other people explaining. That's my profession, my job, as a therapist."

"You should now explain," she says

"I don't want to sound wrong or sick," I say.

"My party lecture at university will make you sick?" she asks.

"There's someone at the university from a long time ago, from San Diego, and I don't want to see her. It's one thing to move here. It's another thing to get close. In fact, I may have moved here to not see her," I say.

"So not see her," Julia says. "But you must meet new people

when you live in new place. I want you to meet people. And you will meet my sister."

I want you to meet people. Is that what's in the storm? I look out toward the mountains. It feels more like wind and rain.

4

Natasha

"Hello! I am bored this evening. I am nice girl who would like to chat with you. Email me at info@NatashaJulia.com and I will reply with my pics."

IT'S IMPOSSIBLE TO TELL NATASHA AND JULIA APART IN THE freezing night rain. Guests are leaving the lecture hall at the university. Some are shaking hands and some are hugging Julia. Umbrellas are opening. Not far from where I'm standing and shivering, Natasha is surrounded by people and calling out to them, "I have joke it doesn't hurt if you keep your thumbs out. This guy must ride across desert. He say to used camel dealer your camel not hold enough water for trip and camel dealer bring camel to water and when camel start to drink, camel dealer take rock in each hand and smashes camel's balls. Camel makes suck sound and sucks up all water woosh like that. Camel ready, camel dealer says. But doesn't it hurt, guy asks, and camel dealer say no, not if keep your thumbs out."

Natasha points her thumbs out with the punch line and Julia, over at the entrance, shouts above the laughter, "Thank you for coming to Russian hospitality birthday lecture party."

Now Natasha and Julia are walking toward me and Natasha says, "I hear you have wonderful house. Does he, Julia? This him?"

"Oh, yes," Julia says. "At base of Cascades is spectacular view home very private acreage sixty-year roof," and Natasha says, "We go there tonight. Maybe we live there." Then she says, "We have mentor doctor in Tacoma. We live in his apartment. Julia got him for us. I make money on internet. I tell people I bored. They pay me not be bored. Julia sells mentor doctor lots of real estate. Where you were tonight? I not see you until now. You not in lecture hall? Why you out here in rain?"

Julia sighs, "Night is pleasant. In Moscow, oh I miss Moscow."

"Not easy to live in Moscow," I offer.

"Yes, is easy!" she says, "Not easy to live on planet."

Natasha says, "Julia conducted Solzhenitsyn presentation. You arrive when everyone leaving. Where you were tonight?"

"I saw pictures," I tell her.

"Pics?" she asks.

"Through a narrow glass in an office door," I say.

"This riddle?" she asks.

"The door was locked, but I saw in," I say. "And the part I saw contained everything decisive for my entire person."

"Like Solzhenitsyn!" she says. "What pics? I have pics. People pay to see my pics."

"I thought it was her sister and her sister's husband. Then I realized it was her."

"Who is her?"

"The one from long ago," I say.

"*That* kind of her," Natasha says and I point, "In that building there," I say.

"Betrayer!" she says and spits on the ground, poking me in the ribs at the same time like an inside joke.

"I got those pictures like a hex sign on a barn," I say. "Her office, her community, her life, her happiness, her security, her purpose, I really didn't want to come tonight. Do you know what I did?"

"What you did?" Natasha whispers.

"I placed my hand on the doorknob so her hand would touch mine next time she enters her office. Time can compress, you know, you can shake it like dice. You can open your hand and bounce time. Then I left the building. I don't know how long I was there. I think I spoke to a secretary."

"When happen?" Natasha asks.

"Right now," I say.

"That where you were for lecture party?" Julia chimes in.

I nod. I ask, "You think I moved here for those pictures?"

"We all move for something," Julia says. "Henry Ford say people want go where never been. When get there, want to come back where they started. That why he invented automobile."

"I see people like ghosts," I tell them. "I can materialize them."

"Everyone can do that," Natasha says.

"But what if I told you Big Larry is standing with us right now?" I ask.

The rain drips off Big Larry's beard. His sander is broken. He holds up his sander to Natasha, but she doesn't see him. She doesn't see the sander. She doesn't see the rain dripping off his beard. She's asking, "Who Big Larry?" and I don't tell her that my cabin floor burned up that little sander of his. He should have rented an industrial one, the kind a person operates standing up. I should have insisted on it. "Still," I say to her, "I should have paid him extra when it burned up."

"What burned up?" she asks.

"Everything, sumac, jade, the sander," I say.

"But those pictures, the ones you see through the door glass in that building, they not burn up like sander? They not hurt?" she asks and I say, "Not as long as I keep my thumbs out."

"Yes," Natasha says. "You keep thumbs out. Maybe we both come live with you on Snoqualmie acreage?"

5

Logging Life

NATASHA KNOWS HOW TO OPERATE HEAVY EQUIPMENT. THERE'S a picture of her nude in Hawaii, piloting an excavator. It hangs in the kitchen above where Julia slices vegetables into small pieces.

"Small pieces," she says as she looks up from the cutting board. "When rain in Seattle, it *really* rain in Snoqualmie. Cascades, those mountains there, stop rain from traveling east and send back to right here. My mother say always cut vegetables in small pieces."

There's a crash on the front deck and she runs onto the porch. Tree limbs hang over the railing. Natasha in her yellow rain gear has felled a maple. She's astride the tree like it's a dead animal, and she yells up at us, "Maple limbs widow-maker. Julia's ex-husband say heavy with moisture. Might drop on you, kill you, widow-maker you." Soon an alder drops. "Had top rot," she yells above the noise of the Stihl Farm Boss. "Might snap in wind and break through bedroom. Now is down."

The hemlock had no taproot. "No taproot might pancake!" she yells.

Logging life is a sudden life. The San Diego sun flashes a sharp spur off Franco's cell phone as he flips it open, shakes it and says, "Damn thing. You say you called?"

Then he says, "I'll do it, but I can't do it now."

"When?" I ask.

"When," he answers and drives off.

"I never have luck with contractors," I say, turning to Marvin the Mobile Mechanic.

"*I'm* a contractor," he says. Then he says, "That guy Franco is a muscle-bound idiot. He could cause damage if taken seriously, and you're taking him seriously. For instance, he broke his wife's nose. She needed plastic surgery. The Mexicans told me. Have you seen her? She's some babe and I'm not kidding."

We walk to where the Mexicans are trimming the old Eucalyptus trees behind the main house. They hang like monkeys from ropes, small chainsaws dangling between their legs.

"Felix screws his wife!" one guy yells, pointing to the road.

"Si, we saw him drive off!" another shouts.

"Is true!" another shouts.

Marvin turns to me. "She's some hot babe and I do mean babe," he says and looks at me closer. "Now I worry for you," he says.

"Everyone's a hot babe," I inform him.

"Oh yeah, since when?" he says.

The main house is pink stucco built on stilts above a giant granite outcropping. You don't see the stilts; they're behind the stucco. The property has many outcroppings and there's an old wooden stilt-structure on several of them. But the main house got the stucco. The property has cactus gardens, mortaros and fields of aloe. Huge green hummingbirds fly up from Mexico, hover above the aloe and suck from the red flowers. The original town water tower sits next to the pink stucco main house and the Historical Society of Crest sometimes brings people in a school bus to look around. They're usually old. Most are committed to gardening. Marvin the Mobile Mechanic returns to the garage, which is also pink stucco, and Franco's wife drives up. He points to where I am up in the main house.

Franco's wife owns the tree trimming company. She's sitting on my bed, looking up at me while I'm searching for the contract in my dresser drawer, and she says, "I can see you were looking at my face. He moved my nose to my ear. Even after surgery you can see it's not right. Do you know Felix?"

I nod. I know Felix.

She says, "His parents died when he was ten and he took care of his eight brothers and sisters by himself and they all grew up and none of them died. Could *you* have done that?"

Her eyes are soft.

"You raised his stock," I tell her. "The guys all know you screwed him. Who knows where things like this go. I can see you're in love. There's a gauntlet love must travel. I traveled mine."

"Did you make it through?" she asks.

She shifts her position and looks out to the road. "I don't know why I married a Tarzan," she says. "It was fun at first. Big strutting guy everywhere we went. Now it's stupid. I should have married a geek. My girlfriend says they're the best in bed and they all have money."

"And there it is, your world view," I say, handing her the contract. "The fence I was promised needs to be built or I can't pay for the tree trimming. I really don't have a choice because I can't live being had. At least, I can't live free if I don't stick up for myself in the face of being had. You understand that concept, don't you? You're a smart woman. You own your own company. Better yet, you get paid to work outside. But you honor me by giving up your secrets, and I want to respect that. You need a plan. You need to divorce your husband and get him out of the business. You need to do it in such a way that he disappears from your life. Then you need a plan to have Felix propose to you so you can save face with the crew because he's been bragging to them. I can help you with that plan. You can be my patient. We can trade sessions for this tree trimming invoice. Or I can get the fence."

She lifts her eyes.

"The crew likes you," she says smiling. "They told me you cooked for them."

"I make my own hot sauce, the Crest recipe," I say. "See? Its written right here perimeter fence from Eucalyptus branches included in tree trimming fee."

"My husband's a jerk and a liar not always in that order," she says. "I have a restraining order out on him. Want to do some blow, hot looking guy like you?"

"I really just want my fence. Or you can be my patient. I have an opening," I say and she says, "I knew I'd like you."

"Never got that fence," I tell Natasha, "and Marvin the Mobile Mechanic almost got me killed, so there's my luck with contractors."

"I not contractor," she says.

"I know that," I say.

"What you know?" she asks. She splits another round in front of the woodshed. She stops and looks at me. She says, "I move in so now I look places to help you. I help with trees too close to house. Julia also moves in. She said she found you first, so no more mentor doctor in Tacoma. He was pig so now you live with both of us. Maybe Julia find true love someday someone put hand on doorknob too late. You have broadband for me. I only want internet connection."

My fingers are stiff as rebar as she talks. The smell of snow is in the air and darkness is drifting in. I say to my fingers, "Look down landscape. Look up Los Arbores, the way of the souls."

"More light," Natasha says, "is good."

"What's good?" I ask.

She picks up the splitting maul again.

"To cut trees away from house," she says. "Pacific Northwest is not high desert outside San Diego."

"The Mexicans," I say. "They slept outside under the sumac where my property sloped toward El Cajon."

"Now *this* is your property," Natasha says.

The splitting sounds — crack, crack, crack - pick up again and I say, "You can't be a local in Crest unless you hate sumac. Big Larry and Geodesic Joe tried to tell me. It stinks when it goes up like a match. Summer and sumac mean big trouble in Crest. You know what else?"

"What else?" she asks.

"Sumac hides rattlers. You know, rattlesnakes," I say.

"And you understand this? You work on this?" she asks. She tosses aside the splitting maul and squares up to me. "I move in with you. My sister moves in with you. No more mentor doctor in Tacoma. Tomorrow Julia takes mentor doctor to opera so I get belongings from apartment."

"You and Julia are moving in," I say and she says, "But you don't ask why? I keep waiting and you don't ask why."

6

Port Angeles

THERE'S A CERTAIN BREED OF PERSON WHO TRAVELS WEST TO chase the sun into the ocean. You could follow that sun too, except then you'd be heading east and you'd be a different breed. So you stand begrudgingly on the edge of the continent, watching the sun dip into the ocean, then you turn and start looking to make a life.

Julia, Natasha and I are off the continent and on a ferry to Bainbridge Island.

Julia says, "Heading west is freedom-like and crossing water is a spiritual metaphor."

Natasha stares at the Puget Sound. Eventually she says, "Our friend Gary dove off ship near Dutch Harbor after wife divorced him and married his best friend. He gained a hundred pounds and didn't float."

Julia says, "Gary is romantic story," and Natasha says, "Julia sees everything as if through lens of university thesis." Later she says, "I always think of Gary when crossing water."

A seagull flies along our line of sight at the speed of the ferry.

Natasha says, "It looks like bird not moving. See Mount Rainier moves behind it. Gary is in bird."

"Here's to you, Gary," I say to the bird.

"He got tricked," Julia says. "Life tricked him so he had to leave."

The bird pulls away like a jet peeling out of formation. I place my arm on the ferry's deep windowsill. It's a long way to Port Angeles.

"Always first time going longer time than first time coming back," Julia says and Natasha says, "Some Seattle people never go to peninsula. How not go? Mountains are like magnets. See them every day. How not feel pulled?" Then she slams her hands to her thighs and shouts, "Bullshit Bingo! How you play like this," and Julia shouts, "Open door policy!"

"Bullshit!" Natasha shouts. Then she whispers, "You go to meeting. Someone says what's on this paper, you shout."

"Synergy!" Julia shouts.

"Bullshit!" Natasha shouts.

"ROI!" Julia shouts.

"Bullshit!" Natasha shouts.

"Alignment!" Julia shouts.

"Bullshit!" Natasha shouts.

"Win-Win!" Julia shouts.

"Bullshit!" Natasha shouts.

"User friendly!" Julia shouts

"Bullshit!" Natasha shouts.

"Big picture!" Julia shouts.

"Bullshit!" Natasha shouts.

"No-brainer!" Julia shouts.

"Bullshit!" Natasha shouts.

"Empowerment!" Julia shouts.

"Bullshit!" Natasha shouts.

"At the end of the day!" Julia shouts.

"Bullshit!" Natasha shouts.

"Bingo!" Julia shouts.

The ferry begins to glide into the Bainbridge terminal and we walk down the metal stairs toward the Explorer. At the bottom of the stairs, a man holds the door open and reviews Natasha for a flaw he won't find, then seems doubly dumb-struck when Julia passes.

I climb into the back seat and Julia gets behind the wheel. Natasha lifts herself into the passenger seat and says, "I look in cars for mirror things."

Julia gets excited. "I write article on car precious religiosity," she says. "The things people find car precious can fill museum. All hang on wall on rear-view mirrors. Maybe I do presentation in PowerPoint at symposium."

The ferry docks with a thud.

"See? Everything is university thesis with her. She is anthropologist assistant professor realtor," Natasha says to me.

Workers pull ropes and gulls squawk. The car in front of us moves. Julia steps on the gas and the Explorer bounces from ferry to asphalt. Immediately the road climbs from a hint of a town into a suburb, soon across a high bridge then along Poulsbo strip malls, a casino, a Fresh Crab cardboard sign, a nailed-shut fireworks shack, and Highway 305 becomes Highway 3.

Julia chants, "No more mentor doctor. No more fat yellow toenails."

Later she says, "See all those highway houses people forsaken for choosing wrong life. See failed machinist shop. Look rusted junk. See broken mobile home still someone living in."

"Make bad choices end here," Natasha says.

"Or with mentor doctor in Tacoma," Julia says.

"Better than logger husband deer meat," Natasha says.

"No talk now. Hood Canal Bridge," Julia says.

Halfway across the bridge, Natasha whispers in a deep voice, "You're going deeper now."

I look down into the Hood Canal far below. The water is moving swiftly. It makes me dizzy. I focus on the end of the bridge.

"You're going deeper now," Natasha repeats in that deep voice.

The voice seems to bounce off the Olympic Mountains, somehow close yet distant and looming at the same time. But it's not Natasha's voice. It's the voice of a hidden giant. The giant is water, mountain, forest and fiord. It's the Hood Canal current and salmon and clams and geoducks and cougars and elk and eagles. The giant is fishing and clamming and hunting and rivers and timber and glacier. Natasha whispers in her deep voice, "You're going deeper now" along Highway 104. Soon it's Highway 101. Civilization appears in a once-farm, a hint of a homestead, and the giant slips off in a game of hide-and-seek.

"We're skirting," Julia says.

Second-growth trees border the highway. Roads to the right lead off to unseen places like Port Townsend and Fort Worden.

"See that!" Julia shouts as a red-tailed hawk caught in a parabola of a longer maneuver enters and leaves the slice of highway sky in front of us. Then pop, we're out of the trees and into Sequim.

"Costco," Julia says. "Farmland now retirement condos, can't trust isolated communities, will turn on you. But see? Dungeness Spit reaches out into water like tongue."

Natasha pivots back to me.

"Tongue," she says.

"Road to Port Angeles," Julia says and Natasha turns forward. "Victoria. Canada. There," she says.

Julia starts to chant, "Burger King, Chinese restaurant, Japanese restaurant, Mexican restaurant, surf-'n-turf, under-a-dollar, bakery, birthday Piñatas."

"Jetsam," Natasha says.

A turn, a turn, a turn, and Highway 101 becomes Highway 112, and Natasha whispers in her deep voice, "You're going deeper now," and soon we cross the Elwa River and it seems the giant is behind us and ahead of us.

"We are *in* the giant," Natasha says then starts chanting, "Grandfather! Grandfather!" and we drop down to the water, to a beach and a circling eagle, and Julia parks and consults her iPhone.

7

Warren

JULIA IS TEXTING FURIOUSLY WITH HER THUMBS. "OKAY," SHE
says finally, "I tell Phil McPherson we attend tea ceremony and
in fact we here. He says cross creek, drive uphill, turn right,
fourth gravel road."

But instead of driving on, she gets out of the Explorer and
stands in a sun spot, zipping up her jacket. The wind blows off her
hood when she points the iPhone at a lone coyote moving through
the tall winter grass. Snap! Picture.

"We sneak up on it!" she whispers with the wind.

I smell the dry grass and sand on my pants as we crawl.

Julia whispers, "Coyote too smart. Nose sees. Already gone that
why it coyote."

"No. Not gone," Natasha whispers back.

Julia pops to her feet. "See? No coyote!" she yells and starts
high-stepping through the winter grass until she's on the beach
almost thirty yards away where rivulets of river water flow into the

sea. She seems surrounded by water, jumping from island to island like some giant estuary goddess.

Natasha and I are still sitting on the ground in the tall grass and she whispers, "When we live here long ago when Julia married we sit here talk secrets. So what do you think of peninsula?"

"Harsh place," I say. "Spend a lifetime breaking your back to survive."

"Now have television and electricity," Natasha whispers.

"Good place for witness protection," I say.

"Funny you say that. Know what is main industry? Correctional institutions, once was logging now everyone employed in prison."

"I rest my case," I say.

"So, yes," she says, standing. "Beautiful places have secrets."

"Like you," I say and she says, "Now you sweet man."

In the distance a bald eagle circles Julia and she yells at us, "Surrogates to sense of community. That name of new PowerPoint presentation."

The eagle glides off to a land stack.

Julia yells, "Peninsula girls meet at beach. Surrogates! Cold I go to car."

Natasha says, "We should catch up so she does not feel alone. Things happen when she feels alone. How we end up two and one when we are three?" So we splash across the rivulets, bouncing up several times to the sand bars as we try to meet up with her, but we don't make it. We almost catch up as she gets in the Explorer. We bounce in just after she starts the engine.

The main road curves away from the Strait of Juan de Fuca and Julia counts two, three, four gravel roads. For a moment, we don't see the water or Canada. The trees close in then open to a red farmhouse. Julia parks in the circular driveway beside a Chevy S-10 with a tall, long-haired Indian sitting on its tailgate drinking a Bud Light.

"No one here," he says.

"Are you Frank Sid?" Julia asks, sticking her head out the

window. Then she turns to look back down the driveway.

"What you lookin' at?" he asks.

"I looking what you looking," she says and he says, "I'm lookin' at you pullin' in."

"I here," she says.

"Want a beer?" he asks.

He crunches his can and tosses it in the back of the pickup. It rattles next to another can.

"Is this Frank Sid's place, friend of Phil McPherson?" Julia asks.

The tall Indian stands.

"You here for the circle?" he asks.

"Yes, we here for ceremony," Julia says and Natasha gets out on the passenger side. They both go to the farmhouse. I stand by the Indian.

"*You* want a beer?" he asks.

He has deep pox marks in his cheeks. He catches my stare and says, "Not all braves are beautiful. See? Look down there. Three cars seven people are coming. I know the cars. I know the people. There's your Frank Sid. It's a caravan. Everyone arrives carrying something. You're carrying something. I know. I am too. Hey, how did you get those two hot broads?"

8

Tea Ceremony

THE TALKING STICK MOVES FROM PERSON TO PERSON AROUND the circle. I'm sitting on the living room carpet between Natasha and Julia. Everyone is cross-legged. A girl across from me stares like a burrowed animal sticking her head out of a hole. Her eyes torch me, because I'm across from her. The talking stick is in her hand. She thrusts it to the carpet and says, "We have drunk the mushroom plant spirit. We pray for safe passage."

Frank Sid turns from stoking his woodstove and says, "Ah-ho!"

"Ah-ho!" everyone says.

"Plant spirit?" I whisper to Julia.

"We drink psilocybin," she says.

"It was psilocybin?" I whisper. "I thought it was *tea!*"

"Tea ceremony," she says.

The talking stick enters Phil McPherson's hand and he says, "The talking stick moves clockwise. When it enters your hand, you will speak holding its base to the carpet. No one speaks but the holder."

He's looking at me because I can't sit up. I'm swallowing hard and often, and I'm trying to keep my balance. But I'm leaning on Natasha and my chest is constricting.

Phil McPherson starts drumming while holding the talking stick up with his toes. I am definitely having trouble sustaining. The more he drums, the tighter my chest constricts. He's singing something now, but it feels very far away. I can see that he looks interested in what he's doing, but I just can't focus outward anymore. All my effort is in breathing. I can't catch a full breath.

Phil McPherson passes the talking stick to Warren.

Warren says, "I don't understand this. Getting the feeling of being drunk to talk about things we talk about anyway. Hey, you," he says to me, "How did you get those two hot broads?"

The talking stick moves from Warren to Frank Sid.

He's bald with black, hairy arms. He's trying to talk but can't. He can't even ah-ho. His mouth opens and closes like a fish gasping for water. His eyes bug out. A sound comes from his mind that can't find the correct part of his tongue.

I can't breathe at all now. I'm in a desperate place. I look up. I try to sit up. Natasha has the talking stick and I lean off of her.

"We with him so we protect him," she says about me. "He our mentor doctor," she laughs, and as she laughs her hair falls over the talking stick.

"Hold the stick steady so we can focus on it," Phil McPherson tells her.

"Bingo," Julia whispers to me from my other side.

I understand now. It's important to focus on the talking stick. I find a small breath and then another. Then I find a big one, that breath that fills your lungs and pulls you through.

I must be hallucinating because everyone is digitized and Julia is laughing and Natasha is laughing and I don't know why they're laughing when the talking stick enters my hand. Ten hours later, we're on a hike and Warren says, "That was funny what you said."

"What did I say?" I ask.

"You said the woman who stopped loving you is called Swims with Horses. You said that's what you call her."

"I didn't say that. I wouldn't," I say.

"Oh, yes," he says, and we turn a bend in the trail and begin to climb. "I know because it reminded me of a joke," he says. "When a Jewish American Princess marries an Indian, she gets an Indian name. We call her White Fish. So I know you said Swims with Horses because I thought White Fish."

"I would have said her name. I'm not afraid to say her name," I tell him.

"What's her name?" he asks.

"I don't say her name," I say.

"Swims with Horses," he says and I say, "Well she liked to swim with horses. She asked me once if I'd ever done that. She said it was a sensual experience."

Warren's black hair shines as he enters a sun spot. He says, "You said she wanted to buy half a horse."

"Maybe she wasn't so hungry?" I say and he says, "You said her schedule didn't permit her to ride as much as she liked. That is as much as was good for the horse. You said you asked her which half of the horse she wanted to buy."

"Well, I thought it was just regular tea," I say. "And I really never say her name."

We're hiking along a ridge now and Warren says, "You didn't spill your guts but I heard you, Man. That's the talking stick once it gets going. The slower things get the more you remember and pretty soon it all blabs out."

"What blabs out?" I ask.

"The critical issue," he says.

"What's that?" I ask.

"Swims with Horses," he says.

"I didn't say that," I say.

"Oh, yes, Man," he says. "You're here because of her. You

said so. A person can travel a thousand miles and still not get any closer. You said that too. You knew she moved on. You're just the custodian of what once was, you know, like a midnight janitor in an empty gymnasium. Hear that sound *hmmm*? That's the light bulbs. How many years listening to those light bulbs? Know what *hmmm* spells? It spells after she's gone."

"I blabbed that?" I ask.

"Worse," he says.

"What's worse?" I ask.

"Cats," he says. "Roxanne had cats, so you couldn't breathe."

"Roxanne didn't have cats. Teresa had cats," I say.

"But you could breathe around Swims with Horses, right? So you swam toward her air hole, found her, anyway found pictures on a wall, and that's how you filled in the missing story she hid from you after she stopped loving you," he says.

"I would never say that," I say. "It's still filtering through me so how could I even understand to say that?"

"Oh yes, Man, you blabbed. Nothing to filter," Warren says. "All resolved with no missing pieces. Now the glow of truth is on you. This has been your journey. You can't get glow of truth from a distance."

"What you guys talk, you new friends?" Julia asks squeezing between us as the trail narrows and Warren is forced to the ferns on the edge of a bluff that drops a thousand feet to kayakers in the Strait of Juan de Fuca. The kayaks are bright yellow. A king salmon's white belly flaps as it surfaces bait. Warren struggles to regain his balance in the ferns and Julia says, "Cold before we walk."

"You and your sister protect this guy from what?" Warren asks.

"Maybe from you," Julia says and we stop where the trail descends toward the sea.

Below us Frank Sid wearing a welder's cap looks like a Taliban.

Warren asks, "Where are the rest of the people from the circle?"

"Went home," Natasha says, catching up to us.

"That's what I mean," Warren says. "This isn't ceremony. No

more mushroom nothing for me."

"The end of the talking stick," Julia says.

"Goes to the carpet," Natasha says.

"See?" Warren says. "Everyone goes home. Entertainment is done. Maybe stop for latte."

"Yes, *latte*," Julia says and Warren says, "I heard a cell phone ringing in ceremony last year. The whole world has gone tourist and I'm not surprised because it's just another infiltration. And you think you're protecting him from me?"

Natasha touches my hand. I look at where she's touching me and I'm still holding the talking stick to the carpet.

"You not say anything," she whispers.

"White Fish," I mutter and pass the talking stick.

9

Visits to Issaquah

Man accused of killing his psychotherapist with a meat cleaver finally arrested.

SNOW MIXES WITH RAIN. SLUSH IS EVERYWHERE AND A BELLEVUE municipal bus launches filth at the used car lot where Natasha stares at the Avanti on the car carrier and the trucker looks at my paperwork.

"Kind of screwed up on the far side, only ever seen one, I mean an Avanti," the trucker says. "Too bad it's messed up."

"It actually got fixed," I tell him.

"Like a dog gets fixed?" he asks.

"No, a cat," I say. "Fixed like the brakes work and it's drivable."

"It is that," he says, backing it down the ramp. "I told my son I have an Avanti on the rack. He's a car enthusiast. He was impressed. He knew all about Raymond Lowey, the Kennedy coins,

Studebaker. I must've raised him right, huh?"

The keys are in my hand. I turn from the trucker to the salesman.

Natasha says something to him in Russian.

He says to me, "Ten thousand to you. You don't care what I make. I call if sold," and I hand him the keys.

"He puts on Craig's List," Natasha says as we walk across the car lot to the Explorer. "He sells all our cars even Armenians he sells for them. Now see all is gone."

"What gone?" Julia asks.

"Gone from San Diego," Natasha says. "Everything is now here."

"He here now," Julia says, "Baba Ram Das."

"*Be* here now," Natasha says.

"I know. I make joke," Julia says.

We get in the Explorer. Julia drives onto the freeway. I lean against the window in the back and stare at the slushy day. Lake Sammamish on the left is gray. Issaquah is on the right.

"I've been visiting Issaquah," I say to Big Larry and he tries to respond but he's having trouble since his stroke.

"Waaaaiiii?" he asks, leaning forward in his motorized wheelchair.

"Dreaming," I say.

He swivels one way then the other.

I say, "Nice job on the floor."

"Hun... red... years... old," he says.

Marvin the Mobile Mechanic walks in, takes one look at Big Larry and says, "Get me some turtle soup and make it snappy!"

"You... crack... me... up," Big Larry says. Then he points at me and says, "Vis... its... is... a...quah."

"Told me," Marvin says. "Found her number on the internet. Now he's bought five acres up there."

Big Larry says, "If I... kicked... him... in... the... balls... he'd... have... *two* acres."

"Say Jacaranda, Larry," I say and Big Larry says to Marvin, "H-h-h-his... fav...or...it... tree."

"Tree," I say, staring at Lake Sammamish.

Marvin the Mobile Mechanic rushes into the kitchen. "What the *f* happened to *him*?" he demands and Big Larry's wife cuts herself chopping cilantro. "Oh, look at that," she says to her finger.

Roxanne hands her a paper towel and says to Marvin, "He had a stroke on the operating table." Then she takes Big Larry's wife's hand because Big Larry's wife isn't doing anything with the paper towel and wraps it around her finger, pressing the other fingers together and folding them into a fist, saying to Marvin, "Don't go to Kaiser unless you want to die."

Big Larry's wife lets out a whimper.

"Don't worry about me, Man. I don't have insurance," Marvin tells her and Big Larry's wife suddenly says, "But they sent him home too soon. We didn't know he'd had a stroke."

"That's what the *f* happened to him?" Marvin asks and Big Larry's wife keeps staring at her fist.

I keep staring at Lake Sammamish.

"Gray day so beautiful," Julia says.

Natasha turns to me. "What *you* see?" she asks.

"I see beautiful gray," Julia answers for me. "All those shades I should be painter."

Pink Floyd blares from the boom box. Marvin the Mobile Mechanic is in the garage under the Avanti and he screams as his knuckles scrape the exhaust pipe. Big Larry chuckles and Marvin yells, "I swore I'd *never* work flat on concrete again!"

"Mo-*mobile*... mech...an...ic," Big Larry reminds him.

"I can't afford my own garage," Marvin says, poking his head out from under the wheel. "Not when I'm trading for whatever I'm trading for here, therapy?"

Big Larry says. "I saw a ratt...ler... yes...ter...day... where... your... head... is. It... was... a... big... juicy rattler." He turns to me. "What... will... you... do... when... all... hope... is... gone?"

"It's never gone. It's an unwarranted perception," I tell him.

"What... is?"

"Everything is," I say and he turns to Marvin. "You... lost... your... mo...tiv...a...tion," he says, pointing at the concrete.

"What?" Marvin demands.

"That!" Big Larry says.

"What's that?" I ask.

"See it," Big Larry says.

Roxanne walks toward us with chips and salsa. She also has Pacifico with limes and tacos Crest style. She places them on the dowel next to the tools. Marvin slides out from under the Avanti and Big Larry says, "Mar...vin's... not... hung...ry." Then he slumps to one side in his wheelchair. It's the most talking he's done in months. He's worn out.

Roxanne puts her hand on his shoulder, "What are you guys talking about?" she asks.

"Why he's leaving," Marvin says.

"He's leaving because I have a new boyfriend I met at church," Roxanne says.

"You do?" I ask.

"Yes," she says.

"Little secrets," I say and Julia says, "Yes, gray clouds so mysterious."

"That not what he says," Natasha tells her and Julia says, "You make us fight over interpret you."

"I not fight," Natasha says and the Explorer begins to climb away from Issaquah toward Fall City. There are thick trees along the road and I say, "This is how I dreamed about heading toward Issaquah. In my dream the road to Issaquah looked more like the road leaving Issaquah. It climbed into the trees like we're doing now."

"Well you never been there when you dreamed there," Natasha says. "It was dream based on telephone number. I make people dream like that on internet."

There's a small town ahead. I don't know if it's Issaquah. I stop for directions at a gas station attached to a humble convenience store like the humble convenience store near Mount Cuyamaca. I begin to ask a woman for directions, but I'm suddenly far away looking back down at me talking to her.

"I'm glad *those* dreams are over," I say to Natasha and Julia drives down the Fall City dip where cops hide.

10

Buster

Start with someone doing something important...
—Advice from a literary agent

BIG LARRY IS POLISHING THE CABIN FLOOR. HE'S ON HIS KNEES and buffing his way toward the exit. Roxanne is watching him from inside the main house. She says to me, "A Santa Ana is blowing in and Marvin told me Buster is missing. Rottweilers are like black bears. They'll turn on you."

"Not Buster," I say.

"But watch out for Marvin," she says.

Big Larry suddenly starts waving frantically and we run to the cabin.

"Grand opening," he announces, stepping aside. "Now you can do whatever you do in here. Start with Marvin. Double up on his therapy. There's a lifetime project. Hope I put down enough varnish."

Marvin rubs his left sock along the floor. He touches the side of his face with his spatula thumb. "How about this one?" he says, "Doctor, nobody pays attention to me and the doctor says next. Or an ugly fat woman complains about stomach pains and the doctor says take off your clothes, stand by the window and stick out your tongue. She stands there naked and asks doctor how will this help my stomach? He says it won't. I'm mad at my neighbor. That's all we are - iterations on a theme. You see my iterations but you don't get my theme. So why should I keep trading you therapy for fixing your car? And I haven't seen Buster in two days. He hides under those filthy blankets at Joe's, but I haven't seen him come out."

"Then why don't you ask Joe?" I ask.

"Buster belongs to Joe's son who's in Afghanistan so it's none of my business," Marvin says. "Buster gets stored at Joe's. And people don't volunteer information to me. And I don't live here. But it bothers me. You know what else bothers me? People screwing me over disguised as dissatisfaction with my work. This girl in Victoria, we were in the same rock band except she had property and I agreed to fix her house in trade for living there. Kind of like a partnership. Like me and you, except she was a chick so I never saw it coming. I sold my instruments after she kicked me out. I ended up Jeremiah Johnson after the Indians killed his wife and son, when he burned down the cabin with their dead bodies inside, and he just rode off. So that's what I did. I burned down my cabin with me in it. And I just rode off. And now I'm Jeremiah-Johnson-after-the-burning for the rest of my life, running away from whatever already caught me. I'm going over there to see if Buster is okay. Hey, wait a minute. Is this a session? Does this count as a session?"

"We've doubled up. So, yes," I tell him.

"Then you need to take notes or I'll feel cheated," he says.

I say, "You might consider being cautious around people who don't know this woman of yours. I mean who don't know how she looks or her special ways. They might laugh their asses off at your whining," and he shouts, "What kind of therapist are you anyway?" and I say, "The kind that says fixing my car is more important for you than pondering over something you can't do anything about, that's long gone except for you using it as an excuse for self-destructive behavior. Ah, that felt good. I think *I'll* lie down now."

"That's a lot of crap," he says.

"Then take this," I say. "The logic you're working under is called contrary to fact hypothesis. It's a fallacy. It's a faulty construct. Pre-law students learn about it in argument. Contrary to fact hypothesis means you don't know how it might have been with this girl because it didn't happen. Something else happened. Your life happened. But if it had happened with her it could have been lousy. You might not be happy. You might tire of her insatiable naïve optimism for example. You might leave her. You can't know. It didn't happen. That's why you're working under contrary to fact hypothesis. You believe you would have been happy with her. You believe that's why you're not happy now. There's your theme. I get it. That's usually what whining is. It's contrary to fact hypothesis. Just fix the car."

He slips on his shoes, nods against an internal thought, steps outside the cabin and yells, "Where is Buster?" Then he yells louder, "*Where is Buster?*"

Joe comes straight out of his geodesic dome and walks toward us. His property is fenced and cross-fenced because it's an equestrian setup without horses, but he opens and closes each gate as if he has horses, and, when he gets close to the east fence, he says, "We had to put him down."

Marvin, who's made his way to Joe's fence, stumbles with the news.

Joe says, "He had a swelling at the side of his neck. It got bigger. It was the size of a softball. Vet said he probably got struck by a rattler."

"Buster," I say and Natasha says, "Don't call me Buster, Mister."

Julia repeats, "Buster, Mister," and starts laughing as we pass the Highway 18 exit. Snow is falling hard and I say, "And there went his last best friend."

"Not I your last best friend?" Natasha asks and Marvin says, "Old Rottweiler knew me. I can't explain it."

Joe says, "Well, I seen you visiting Buster, walking to the fence and stepping over these gofer holes to bring him doggy treats. Rattlers use gofer holes as pathways. You've been walking over rattlesnakes."

Marvin's fists open and close and Julia takes the Snoqualmie exit.

"Look, elk," Natasha says. "See how thick like horses. Look now there's big one with antlers?"

"It's a herd," Julia says. "I slow down even more so not smash your truck. I see them jump on road."

"We so lucky," Natasha says, "only twenty-seven miles from downtown and in elk."

II

HIPPO EATS DWARF

BANGKOK: A hippopotamus swallowed a circus dwarf
in a "freak accident" in Northern Thailand, according to
a columnist in the Pattaya Mail. The Grapevine column
reported: "A circus dwarf, nicknamed Od, died recently when
he bounced sideways from a trampoline and was swallowed
by a yawning hippopotamus waiting to appear in the next act.
Vets said Hilda the Hippo had a gag reflex which caused her to
swallow. More than 1000 spectators continued to applaud
wildly until they realized there had been a tragic mistake."

TRUE LOVE WILL FIND YOU IN THE END. IF YOU KEEP LOOKING that's all you have to do because true love is looking too. Natasha gets out of bed and turns up the iPod in its docking station.

"We like this song," she says. "Come see. Swallows dive bomb Julia at garden. Look she is expert squatter. Snow is off top of

Mount Si and gas station man say best moment for planting. Avanti sold. He say sold to retired Boeing guy whose wife not happy about it."

"Well, at least I don't have to order parts anymore from one-eight-hundred-gotcha," I say.

Natasha asks, "What that mean?"

"End of an era," I say. "Another end. Some endings have lots of endings in them. Sometimes you can't get to the end of your endings."

"But spring is here," Natasha says, spinning around joyously, and, at the raised boxes, Julia says, "Warren is coming."

A Chevy S-10 pickup rattles up the driveway and a tall Indian gets out. His long, black hair flows away from his denim shirt. He takes in the scene with a look.

"Hey, Swims with Horses," he says to me. "How did you get these two hot broads? You got them arguing with each other yet? I come for you," he says to Julia and Julia says, "Not walk in garden, Warren, and how you know I'm not my sister?"

At the same time, a grey ghost dog leaps from the back of the pickup and moves along the periphery like a thing here and gone.

"That's Tundra," Warren says to me. "I'm not walking in your garden," he says to Julia.

"So what's my name?" Julia demands and he says, "Julia."

"Wrong!" Julia shouts, pointing at Natasha. "That's Julia. You come for *her*. I am Natasha."

"Okay with me," Warren says. "One hot broad is like another. Actually, they're all like one another. Hey, Swims with Horses, you ready for a Northwest adventure?"

Natasha and I sit in the back of his pickup, facing rear traffic. We huddle in an itchy, stinky blanket that has been around many campfires. Warren, Julia and Tundra the gray ghost dog are in front. Now we're hiking the middle fork of the Snoqualmie far back where the canyons meet in a V and the river bubbles black. Warren picks up a feather, reviews it and discards it, while Julia is called by pebbles, and we all walk in the mist. The air is early spring cold, wet to the touch. Ferns pop up like treble clefs and soon the trail becomes wall-to-wall green. Water explodes upward, curls then disappears. Tundra runs in spasms along the periphery, and we hike up through places untouched by light. Our bodies grow larger. Our hearts pound, our minds speak. Someone says, "A thing." Did someone say a thing or was it just our bodies expanding in these darker places?

Warren says to Julia, "I want to be with you. Isn't that enough?"

"When that enough?" she answers.

"Fine with me because I don't want to be with you," he says. "Who cares? Hippo eats dwarf. It's all just a big yawn. Why aren't you thrilled that someone wants you? And I want you more than I want your sister. That alone should get you."

"Get me? That how you say?" she asks.

"I have the real thing for you. What's the difference how I say it? And you need someone to call you on your crap before you get too caught up in it," he says.

"Bad language strike three," she says.

"I didn't say I was out to succeed," Warren mutters. "Just want us to bother each other for a long time, you know, years."

"You mean bugger for years," she says.

"Hey, who taught you that?" he asks.

"See how bad language is?" she says.

"Hoy-ah," Warren sighs.

Then silence. Step after step the silence given dark places. Warren seems to lope. Julia moves like a dancer even bending under branches. Darkness touches ground. A stream meanders on a carpet. Roots surface like bones. Decay wafts. Tundra reappears. Silence soaks previous talk, precious talk. Natasha is behind me, a sense of her on my back. We stumble upward until we pass into light pools.

Julia says, "What you think about you speak about. What you speak about you bring about. What you think about today, Warren?

Bugger me?" Then she laughs.

Natasha whispers, "See you can't make someone love you."

Warren climbs to where the trail flattens at a lake, and, at the outlet, he reaches into a huckleberry bush and lifts out a red-tailed hawk feather. He hands it to me and says, "The thing about married woman is they like to confess. She's not married is she? Not to you anyway. You want the other one Natasha, right? How do you tell them apart? They're not one thing to you are they? I would have liked to have seen that hawk. That was one big bird. Red-tailed hawks are messengers. Maybe you want the message. Maybe you carry the message."

Julia catches up to us and grabs the feather from me and points it at Warren.

"We know what you mean when you say Hippo Eats Dwarf," she says. "You got fooled. It's a lie. Snopes dot com says practical joke urban legend. Put on internet and news media pick it up. Soon people talk about it to you and you invented it, and big yawn to you, my friend."

Warren turns to me and says, "Don't mess with academics. They're all born dead."

The red-tailed hawk feather almost blows out of my hand in the back of the pickup. Natasha snuggles close under the itchy, stinky blanket.

"Why did Julia return it to me?" I ask and Natasha says, "I Julia."

"Why did you hand me back this feather?" I ask.

"How I know?" she says. "Maybe for your reason."

I hand it to her and she holds it up.

"No, no give it back," I say and she laughs.

"That's how I know you're Natasha," I tell her.

"How you know?"

"Julia would have let it go."

"How soon Warren give up?" Natasha asks. "Maybe he kills her? See the size of his hands? He was in war. That why Julia is in front seat pretending to be me. But Warren does not know difference."

It's dark now and Natasha leans over the kitchen table. "What you making?" she asks, then she says, "Oh, a rattle with a feather in it," and Warren kisses Julia at the front door and Julia says, "You taste like cigarettes. Kiss me again I puke on you."

"Hoy-ah, what a woman," Warren says.

"But of course you *not* delighted what a woman I am," Julia says.

"No, I'm relieved," he tells her. "I had a woman like you once. She got the house and I got a case of the Tourette's."

"You never have house," she tells him.

12

Walking Speckles

MY EX-WIFE IS TELLING ME A STORY BACK IN EL PASO AFTER our divorce.

"I had on my housecoat. You know I always like to wear my housecoat," she's saying. She calls a housecoat something she sleeps in and never gets out of the next day. In her case, it's an ankle-length pink dress with fake pink fur at the wrists. She's wearing it now. "And I was walking Speckles at night, but she shrugged off her collar at the front door, so I was just walking the collar on the leash around this here neighborhood in my housedress and bare feet. And people were running to their windows and calling other people to see, and they were pointing. But I didn't know why because I wasn't looking at Speckles so I didn't know she wasn't there. I didn't know I was just walking the collar. Except when I got home, there she was wagging her tail at me."

"Same furniture," I say and I might have said, "Where did Hank go?" because her new husband had gone into the bedroom.

But I must have said, "Same furniture," because I didn't know what she was saying until the whole thing was out her mouth. But I knew fake fur was flying. She said, "That woman of yours was all over me when I called her. She said you were crazy and I was crazy and she hung up on me. There's your same furniture. And the only reason I called her was to ask how she could do that to you, because you loved her so much, same furniture. And that's who you left me for. That's who you chose, the one who won't have you. She won't have you and she won't have me asking her why when I'm the one you cheated on in the first place, same furniture."

All the furniture in her house is from our divorce, even my trophies, and there is nothing new in the way of furniture. It's all the same in just a different house, in a different state and in a different marriage.

"Is it the same in the bedroom?" I ask and she says, "No, it's *not* the same in the bedroom. That's where you're wrong."

"Well, it was a lovely solid cherry set. And the furniture looks good in here," I say.

"Come, Speckles," she says but Speckles can't get up. She tries and my ex-wife says, "Remember she used to jump this high when you'd say *go for a walk*?"

"I remember," I say and walk into the guest bedroom.

"Remember what?" Marvin the Mobile Mechanic asks, holding up a mousetrap with a caught mouse in it. "Remember what Zarathustra said, I hate killing mice." He steps outside and tosses the mouse across the fence into Joe's yard. "Now I have to wash my hands," he says, coming back into the cabin. "They can get into a place through a hole the size of a quarter. Do you know how? They squish the bones in their heads, and we think we have abilities. But what if the whole is the size of a dime? Depends on the head, Zus spake Zarathustra. What a scorcher out there. It must be over a hundred. I'm not working on the Avanti today. I'm watering the succulents."

He's wearing cut-offs and no top.

He says, "I remember things too. I remember we were making love. I had my torso lifted off her torso because I read somewhere that it's good to keep your weight off women when making love, two-thirds off anyway. When suddenly without missing a beat she pulls herself up to me and squeezes me so I feel the warmth of her breasts. Do you know what I thought at that moment? I thought that someday I'll remember this is me. So there it is. This is me."

"I'm happy for you," I say.

"What's that supposed to mean?" he asks and I say, "It's just a summary we in the profession use to give a false sense of closure."

"Zus spake Zarathustra," he says, holding his chest with both hands.

I hear my ex-wife out in the street calling, "Speckles! Speckles! *Speckles!*" and I reach below the bed and there's Speckles under me.

13

John Davidson Summer Camp for Lead Singers

THE SUN RISES IN THE EAST ABOVE CREST THEN POUNDS DOWN on El Cajon, Spanish for The Box. It splashes long eucalyptus tree shadows on the road down from the municipal water tower where two girls wearing bicycle helmets ride to school on ponies. Big Larry's daughter is one of them, her friend Clara is the other, followed by three dogs. Cactus flowers, blue jacaranda leaves and oleanders, pinks, reds and yellows, sway in the Santa Ana. The giant jades at the entrance to the pink stucco main house appear limp and thin. Some are shriveled and black. You can hear them swell at night when there's moisture, if you wait long enough and listen hard enough. You can always tell what the weather has been by looking at jade, and, for a long time now, the weather has been unbearably hot. Over the hump and down the backside hole that's Harbison Canyon, jackrabbits scurry.

Big Larry says to me, "It's what we do up here in the high desert. We stand in the middle of the road. Hey, if you don't like it, we can pretend to be inspecting the crushed asphalt if anybody asks. But nobody's going to asks. They all know what we're doing. We're road standing. By the way, another thing maybe nobody told you about up here, you've got a small septic. It'll back up on you. Ask Joe. He'll likely come out here once he sees us in the road. Those big tree roots are water-seeking in drought, you know, or maybe you don't know. There's a woman Mary up the street, the house next to the big compost pile, the old girl, seen her, latent-dyke-pretend-biker chick her father owns half of La Jolla? Her septic backed up. A thick twisting eucalyptus root got in her French drain and went all the way up her leach field and grew up her toilet. Diddled her one day when she was taking a poop. Said she jumped so high she almost hit the ceiling. She thought it was a snake. So you can't flush anymore when that happens."

Joe walks over to us with three blackberries in his twisted hand.

Big Larry says, "I was just telling him about his septic."

"Small," Joe says. "Needs sucked once a year. Call that guy with the truck that has the smiling skunk on it and the words *it ain't sweet*."

He holds the blackberries out to me.

"Are these for me?" I ask and he says, "Yes, even though that mechanic of yours makes me jumpy."

"Me too," Big Larry says and he rubs his jaw. "I got this pain. I'm going in for an operation. They say they'll get rid of it. Nick the trigeminal nerve."

"That's brain stuff, isn't it?" Joes asks suspiciously.

"Just nick it, not cut through it," Big Larry says. "A nick, just like this, nick. Nick, that's it."

"They wouldn't be nicking me in the brain," Joe says.

Roxanne drives up holding a bouquet of flowers out the window and she hands it to Big Larry as she passes. Then she turns into the driveway, the Ford Ranger disappearing behind the wilted giant jades. Now she's in the road with us and Joe says, "Here's that beautiful girlfriend of yours. Whatever made *you* so lucky?"

Roxanne, hugging and kissing, melts into the scene the way she does and asks, "What are you guys talking about?"

"Marvin," Joe says.

"Blackberries," I say.

"Septic," Big Larry says.

"Small. Needs pumping," Joe says.

"Where'd you get these flowers?" Big Larry asks and she says, "I got stuck behind a moving house so I picked while I waited."

"It's coming," Joe says.

"There it is," Big Larry says.

A house mover with an old craftsman-style house on its bed negotiates around the corner and rolls toward us. Workmen walk in front and on the side of it with long poles.

"Looks like security for the Pope," Big Larry says.

The lead worker shouts, "May have to cut your trees to get past."

"Not likely!" I call back.

"I don't think you'll have a choice. You may have to trim them," Joe whispers.

"This is a private road run by the water tower authority," Big Larry calls out. "And we're the water tower authority."

"Well, this house is coming through," the lead worker says, reaching us, and Big Larry says, "See if you can pass without busting this guy's trees. He just had them trimmed."

"That's the plan," the lead worker says, walking away and Joe calls after him, "You can move a bit closer to my side of the road if you have to."

"I saw where Marvin lives," Roxanne says.

"The meth house," Big Larry says.

"What are you talking about?" I ask and Roxanne says, "All those cars, it's a billboard."

"He's a mechanic," I say and she says, "Over twenty cars half with their hoods up. None of them work. That's why he walks here. There's a refrigerator in the front yard, if you can call it a front yard. The windows are covered with cardboard."

"He lives there with his aunt," Joe says.

"His brother and his cousin's mother," Big Larry says.

"He has a brother?" I ask and one of the flatbed's big front wheels digs into Joe's side of the road and the house tilts with a creaking sound. The workmen poke their poles up at my trees to free the roof and the roof scrapes past the first set of overhanging branches. Then the house creaks again more violently, a snapping kind of sound, as the flatbed regains the crushed asphalt and the roof scrapes along the second set of eucalyptus branches.

The house rolls on and there's Marvin waving as if he's part of the work crew. We all step back into the middle of the road and watch the house continue toward the water tower.

Big Larry takes Marvin's hands by the fingers and says, "Someone smashed them with a hammer then smashed them again. Then smashed them again and again until they were like flat spoons and that's Marvin."

"Hey, leave me alone," Marvin says, pulling back.

"Roxanne saw your house," Joe says.

"It's not my house. It belongs to my aunt," he says. "I'm just there sometimes. In fact, I'm not really there at all. I'm moving back to El Cajon not that any of you require my itinerary."

"I'll show you the house on our way to O.B.," Roxanne says and Marvin says, "O.B.?"

"We're going on a date," Roxanne tells him.

"You're going to the ocean, to Ocean Beach?" Marvin asks.

Roxanne and I are staring at the ocean down at Sunset Cliffs where Ocean Beach gives way to Point Loma and she's saying, "Last week right out there a Great White bit off this girl's leg and she died. She was only twenty-two and it was her birthday. Know what else? She was in remission from cancer and she was celebrating by skinny dipping. She liked to skinny dip, that's what the paper said, because her friends were interviewed, and the shark must have taken her for a seal. The kelp beds out there aren't safe. There are lots of fish for sharks. That's where we're going."

"I didn't bring a bathing suit," I say.

"We'll swim out there in our underwear. And we'll say a prayer for her," she says.

We walk along the gravel path down from Point Loma Nazarene University and Roxanne is saying something about how to describe this place as the same as it was thousands of years ago, but right here in the middle of the city, and you'd have to start by saying local knowledge.

"She was a student up there," she's saying, pointing at a university building, but other than that building, there is nothing but raw land and seacoast, except suddenly we're walking along a manicured baseball field. From there it's straight down over the dunes to the beach and the caves and Roxanne says, "We'll put our clothes in here," and by in here she means at the back of a cave.

We run out into the foam and start swimming through the breakers. Nobody is here but us. We're treading water now in the middle of the ocean where it's calm. Roxanne says, "Heavenly Father," and I look around.

Roxanne asks, "What are you doing?" and I say, "Waiting for my leg to get bitten off."

"It won't," she says.

"Heavenly Father," Roxanne begins again.

"Did I mention I'm not a very good swimmer? I used to be. There's something slimy touching my legs," I say and Roxanne says, "That's kelp. Don't get tangled in the kelp."

"Is that a euphemism?"

"Just move your feet slowly like you're on a bicycle. You'll tread water."

"Are sharks slimy?"

"No. They're rubbery. Heavenly Father-"

"There was someone before you, someone who killed San Diego for me. I need you to know that," I say. "If not for you, I could never leave here. What we have has broken me even with this place."

"Let me say this prayer. You believe in God don't you?" she says.

"I just want you to know that you're perfect," I say.

"Heavenly Father, bite off this guy's leg."

"Hey, He can hear."

"Then you do believe."

"I have a policy not to deny God in water."

"Then let me say my prayer. Heavenly Father, we are here for such a short time."

"She said she decided not to change her life and all I could say was you haven't even heard me play guitar and she said yes I have."

"Bless this place. Bless this girl you have taken to your heavenly home, this girl who suffered in her young life."

"She had a cheap nylon string guitar and I picked it up once to play but it was out of tune so I started tuning it then gave up and that's what she called having heard me play guitar."

"Bless the soul of this girl who loved fun and never complained and who swam out to celebrate her birthday. Thank you for keeping her forever happy in your home for eternity. Amen."

"Amen," I say and Roxanne says, "What was that?"

"What was what?" I ask.

"What you were saying?"

"At summer camp the counselors smeared Crisco on us so we could swim Lake Memphremagog end to end. The counselors were in rowboats. I was ten but I really haven't been a good swimmer since."

"Actually it was something about you leaving San Diego, some convoluted logic about a guitar?"

"I blab sometimes when I'm under stress. I wouldn't be good under torture. Show me tongs. I blab."

"You'd turn in your buddies?"

"No. I'd lie quickly."

"Why is that not comforting? Someone from work asked me out. Should I tell him I have a boyfriend or not? Let's body surf to shore."

Roxanne and I are deep inside the cave. She's pulling on her shorts and I'm watching the ocean out the far end of the cave as if through a canon. She says, "I became a born again Christian. I love Jesus. He died for our sins. What's your religion?" and I say, "I'm not a fan of team sports."

"I'll pray for you," she says and I say, "I'm not denying Spirit. Maybe dogma brings you closer to it? I'm not convinced, but maybe it does. I think you're luckier than the rest of us. You're so beautiful. If you have a compulsion to pray, pray for Marvin."

"I can do that," she says.

We're walking along the beach. The waves crash the shore. The sun beats on the brown hills of what California used to be. Roxanne says, "I want to know about this woman who messed you up, who is messing us up."

"A little push goes a long way with me," I say.

"Am I pushing you?" she asks and I say, "That's why she said we were through just before I begged her that she hadn't even heard me play guitar."

"Then just tell me one story," she says and I say, "We went into a restaurant near Mount Cuyamaca and a guy with hair down to his ass was wearing a T-shirt that said John Davidson Summer Camp for Lead Singers and it was so funny that I wanted to buy that shirt right off his back but I didn't even say great shirt. I didn't want to do anything except watch myself from far away."

"That's your story John Davidson Summer Camp for Lead Singers?"

"It plays out differently in my head."

"How does it play out in your head?"

"It plays out fully."

"What do you mean fully?"

"The before, the after, the complexity of the during, what was in the left corner of the restaurant, what was behind the counter, you know, all that now stuff that keeps sitting in now."

"Even now it sits in now?" she asks.

"It's always in now," I say.

"So tell me all of it," she says and I say, "If I told you every detail you wouldn't like me and I wouldn't know the moment you got bored."

"But how would you come out?" she asks.

"Come out?" I ask.

"Yes. How would you come out?" she says.

"You mean look?" I ask.

"I mean how would you come out with every detail of your inner world with her, just like it is in your head? What would be your animation character? Would you be a snake or a lion? How would you look to me?" she asks.

"Good. I'd look good to you but only because you see me now," I say.

"Only?" she asks.

"No. I guess not," I say.

"We should go to Cuyamaca," she says.

"You would do that for me?" I ask.

"We could take Marvin," she says and I say, "I can't talk about Marvin because he's my patient."

"He's not your patient," she laughs. "He's your mechanic. You can't turn all your neighbors into patients."

"No, he's my patient," I say. "In fact, he's my only patient. I had lots of patients once. I had a practice. I had nurses and physician assistants. I was connected to that hospital where Big Larry is getting his operation."

"What happened to all that?" she asks and I say, "I can't talk about it," and she says, "Unless you're blabbing under stress. We're on a date. People talk about themselves on a date. You have to do that. It's normal."

"You want people to be normal, so do I," I say. "Not simple, not ordinary, normal. Doctor Milton H. Erickson talks about happy, productive, future-looking, normal people. They can't help but be humorous about themselves in specific and the world in general, and I like Milton Erickson."

"So what's wrong with Marvin?" she asks.

"I'll tell you something about that but then you must help me as a consulting therapist. That will make this a professional consult. Okay?" I ask.

"Okay," she says and I say, "I have a friend in British Columbia down from Nelson in a town called Sirdar. It's basically not a town. It's a tavern on a highway. People who don't know Sirdar know the Sirdar Bar. Most people only know the two words together. Near closing time some local rotates his finger and that's the signal for everyone to go outside and stand in the middle of the highway to sample the latest crop of marijuana. So everyone is drunk and stoned come one in the morning and most people just walk home through the forest or up the freeway. My friend and I were walking back to her house and she had a flashlight pointing at her face instead of in front of her. We could barely see where we were going and I asked her why she pointed the flashlight at herself and she said so cougars could see how big she was. That's what's wrong with Marvin. He's pointing the flashlight in the wrong direction. He's behaving off a false theory."

"So what are you doing for him?" she asks.

"I'm trying to get him mad at me," I say.

"So he'll do what?" she asks.

"Point the flashlight at me. Then maybe he'll just keep pointing it outward," I say and she says, "Why not just get him a puppy named Buster? What happened to you?"

"I don't want to talk about me. You don't want me to talk about another woman. We were married but not to each other and we were catching moments trying to make them add up, but I don't think things add up that way. You don't get the whole person by summing pieces. Maybe that's why she didn't know I played guitar. Talk to the old timers."

"What about the old timers?" she asks and I say, "Old timers tell you it doesn't happen all at once. I mean climbing back out of a hole, becoming a good citizen. It doesn't just snap back into place."

"What doesn't just snap back into place?" she asks.

"Things that slip off you, things like Peace on Earth," I say.

"Goodwill toward Men," she says.

"Yes, that's it," I say. "That's the desired outcome. It's goodwill toward everyone and everything, reflected in how you feel about yourself. Every self-promoting phony has a package to get you healed. When I leave San Diego I'm not taking San Diego with me. But in the meantime I've been working toward getting whole. I was willing to wait forever until everything was wonderful enough to leave."

"Is there a wonderful enough to stay?" Roxanne asks and I say, "Are we having a good date yet?"

"Only if you're my boyfriend," she says. "Or is it because I'm religious?"

14

First Line of Defense

Know your past, look at your condition.
Know your future, look at your actions.

THE PLAY IS IN THREE PARTS. PART ONE: THE SURGEON EXPLAINS to Big Larry's wife how well the operation went but something is off in the nurse's expression.

The surgeon says, "We found the plastic wedge from the previous operation and removed it."

The surgeon is tall and in her space. He looks down on her. His smile is practiced, pasted on, and I can't get my eyes off his nurse but she won't look at me. She stares at Big Larry's wife. I've seen that stare before. She's looking for a sign that Big Larry's wife doesn't believe what she's hearing. But there is no sign. The nurse keeps looking for it though. The air just feels wrong.

The surgeon says, "It went well. We nicked the trigeminal nerve, just a little nerve nick, and that should get rid of his jaw pain. He's waking up now in Intensive Care."

Big Larry's wife is a telecommunications executive but she has that arts and crafts Crest look. Now she humiliates herself.

She says, "Yes, poor guy all the pain he's dealt with," and she says this to the butcher in pajamas who slipped up inside her husband's brain.

And here is the nurse watching with worried eyes. Maybe she recognizes me and that's why she won't look at me. Always leave room for your own doubting. A piece of you must always consider that the rest of you is wrong, so best to go see Big Larry in Intensive Care. But this scene doesn't look good and doesn't feel good. Meanwhile Big Larry's wife is socializing up a storm with the surgeon.

All the way down the hall, my former self looks in on me, glad for me that I've moved on, or recovered, or made it back, or wherever I am, but knowing this is where my skills belong.

Part Two of the play is with Big Larry in Intensive Care and Part Three is a month later road standing with Joe saying, "They fucked him."

"Yep, they fucked him," Joe says.

He kicks at the crushed asphalt, sort of rubs it with his work boot and inspects it to no satisfaction, since there was no question so the answer doesn't forthcome. He nudges it again. "Fucked him," he repeats to the asphalt. "We're just a bunch of backwater nocalutes, you know that? We don't have those gewgaws unrelated to utility. You know those bells and whistles? That's why they fuck us."

"What's a nocalute?" I ask and he says, "Don't know just made it up. We're just figments of each other's imagination. When we're gone, someone else moves into our homes. Others get our things. We all have different pasts but we all share the same future."

"You mean furniture, don't you?" I say.

"What I mean is we're here for each other. Nocalutes get that.

That's a nocalute. We're not here to cover our own asses. He's just been sitting in his damn house, you know that? They got him a wheelchair. I saw it arrive. Tell me what happened to him again."

"He had a stroke on the table but they claim they didn't know it. So they sent him home pretending everything was normal. Then they found out he'd lost his left side," I say.

"And he can barely talk," Joe says. "He lost the learning of it and all because of some pain in the jaw. I bet he'd take that pain back now. So like I was talking about nocalutes, just think of everything as your baby. You know the song when something is wrong with my baby, something is wrong with... *me*. Right! You *knew* it was wrong because a person knows when it's wrong. Something's wrong out there, something's wrong in here," he says, touching his chest. "You didn't need proof then and there. That feeling was proof. Sometimes the proof comes later and sometimes it never comes. But you don't need the proof because the proof comes in the way the thing felt wrong in the first place."

"Are you calling Big Larry my baby?" I ask.

"I'm saying it's nice you're my neighbor," Joes says and he inspects the crushed asphalt a few steps away.

Joe kicks at the crushed asphalt.

"Looks good here too," he says, "Maybe tighter than there."

"Maybe," I say.

"It went down pretty even," Joe says.

After a time, Big Larry's wife rolls Big Larry into the street and leaves him there with us.

Nobody's looking at anybody.

The dry wind picks up.

Big Larry says, "Whaaaa..."

"What?" Joe asks.

"Whaaa...t.... you... do... ing?" Big Larry asks and it takes a long time to get it out and doesn't sound like words.

"Road standing," Joe tells him.

"Mmmmm...eee... too," Big Larry says, then he pokes me with his alive hand. "I'm row...ode.... sit....ing."

"Takes everything I've got to listen to you," Joe says and Big Larry starts to cough.

Finally he says, "Pooooooor.... you."

"Know your past, look at your condition. Know your future, look at your actions," Joe says. "In fact I saw that on a sign in front of the Korean church, the one that used to have why do your feet smell and your nose run," and Big Larry says, "I... have... to... sit... when... I... pee... because... the... doc... told... me... I... can't... lift... any... thing... heavy."

"Talk about heavy," Joe says, "I got a call from Rick's wife down the street except she's out in the wilderness because Rick is in the mountains with his eight-year-old son and the boy apparently shot a bull elk and she wants me to show up because some of the guys are there skinning and gutting it and she's on her cell calling everyone. This is during hunting season, remember. I'm just not into killing elk, but we're friends and I want to be respectful, though it's a bit of a push to ask me to misconstrue my presence as support. I'm a union guy so people think I'm rugged because of my outward appearance."

"You don't look so rugged," I say and Joe says, "Anyway she keeps going into detail about how they got the bull elk strung up in a tree, and I'm getting sick on the description. Then I get emailed these pictures of the magnificent beast with Rick Junior between the antlers, and the kid looks overcome with confliction. That's the difference between Republicans and Democrats. They have to kill a bull elk and we have to fuck a prostitute."

Part Two of the play is in Intensive Care and Big Larry is surprised to see me. His eyes are watery. He smiles up at me. There are some places you don't expect to see a neighbor.

"Hi, Larry," I say.

"There... a...past," he says.

"Don't pick your scab," his wife says. "It's your first line of defense."

15

Bears

JULIA HAS FEATHERS IN HER HAIR AND SHE'S DANCING AROUND me and beating a drum. Warren and I are stretched out on the living room floor with our arms touching. I haven't seen them all summer.

"Warren says, "I see something."

"Soul retrieval working," Julia says.

Warren says, "I see Orcas."

Julia chants, "Orcas, orcas, orcas," and I have to go to the bathroom something fierce. I should be envisioning orcas, pods of them, in the Puget Sound or maybe in Alaska, but I can only think about why I didn't pee before we started this soul retrieval.

After a while Warren says, "I see horses."

Julia chants, "Horses, horses, horses."

"Orcas and horses," Warren says.

The drum beat is making my bladder burst.

Natasha is no help. I sneak a peek at her and she's shaking her head on the couch.

"There's something else," Warren says.

Julia chants, "Hee-anna-heenay-hey-yana."

"Something else," Warren repeats.

Now there is silence, except for the drumming, and except for my need to pee, and except for Warren touching the full length of my left side with his right side as part of the technique to retrieve my soul. I should have peed.

I start dreaming about a conversation I'm having with myself. I'm saying that sometimes I get in a car for a long drive and forget to pee. Two blocks out and I think, "I should have peed." I should have peed when I went looking for Rocky, our parakeet. I'm looking for him because my wife let him fly around the house and he flew out the door. "I should have peed," I say to myself in the car.

"It's not clear," Warren says.

"It's getting clear," Warren says.

"Wolf," Warren says.

Julia gives one final hard strike to her drum.

I wait.

Warren gets up like I'm praying he will. He reaches down to me. I'm on my feet. We are standing there.

"Orcas, horses and wolf - is good," Julia says and I say, "Did you see a parakeet?" and I go into the bathroom to relieve myself.

"Overcome," I hear Warren say. "I've seen it before."

I'm parked in front of Swims with Horses house and I'm drunk. Her husband comes out and knocks on my window. I wake up and have to pee. He says, "What are you doing here?" but I think he's the highway patrolman from eight years earlier outside Odessa, Texas.

"I got tired driving," I say. "So I pulled off the freeway to sleep."

"Where you heading?" he asks.

"Houston to El Paso," I say, "to pick up my wife. Then we're moving to San Diego."

"Well, park under that street light. It's safer there. I can watch you. You could get knifed here in the dark and no one would know until morning," he says.

"What are you doing here?" her husband asks and he has no idea I'm the one who's been making love to his wife, the one she rejected. These are the bad times.

"I got drunk. I'm waiting to get sober so I can drive home to my family," I say, and I realize I'm not in Texas. I'm in San Diego. He's not the highway patrolman. He says, "I can get you a cup of coffee."

"I'll be gone soon," I say.

"I'll be gone soon," Marvin the Mobile Mechanic says.

"Gone where?" I ask.

"To Idiot Town," he says.

"Where's that?" I ask.

"What do you mean where's that? Everywhere is where it is and inside you too, just waiting for you, and you don't *know* what an idiot is until you're in Idiot Town," he says. "Oh, you knew it was getting the better of you. Anyway the line is drawn and has the name it named itself, the line you're crossing. If you keep going the way you're going, you'll be dead or in jail. That's the name of the line."

I say, "There's another thing."

He says, "What is it?"

I say, "It's a truth you can't grasp at the time of the truth."

"What's that?" Marvin asks.

I say, "The only way to recognize the line that names itself is to have already crossed it."

He says, "You're saying I crossed the line because I saw the line?" and I say, "Of course. How else could you see the line?"

"The line that names itself?" he asks and I say, "That's the line you've crossed."

"Can I get back?" he asks, and that's when I realize in a gush of relief that I'm standing in front of the toilet.

When I return to the living room, Julia is putting her drum away in a pillow case. She says, "Got in Wyoming at ecumenical gathering. Damn Sioux made me kill puppy with wooden mallet.

We ate puppy."

Warren says, "I haven't had so much fun since the Clarence Thomas hearings."

"Why you do that? You want to be Indian so much?" Natasha cries. "When in Napoli young boy pinch your ass and you chase him down street yelling. You want to be Italian woman. What you want be next? What then you kill?"

"I not bragging," Julia says and Natasha says, "You beg for karma. You deserve karma. You will get karma."

"No, only people who brag beg for karma," Julia says.

"You killed puppy," Natasha says.

"I didn't see it," Warren says. "I was gathering wood. The Sioux boys converged on her. Some sense of humor those guys. They watched Little Big Man too many times."

"Bears, three of them, walking up gully," Julia says and points.

The bears walk through the foxglove. The neighbor's dogs start to bark incessantly in the distance. The bears don't care. They trudge on deliberate bear-style and top flowers as they climb the gully.

"What a place you live," Julia says.

"Go kill them!" Natasha screams. "Hit with paddle you not my sister."

"There, they're fighting now. I leave her with you," Warren says. "Now you have two hot broads again. I like victims because they make good sex partners. Oh, she's pregnant."

Julia turns to Warren. "If I pregnant I get coat hanger my friend." Then she turns to her sister, "I am social anthropologist. I know more now than before. I give presentation soon at university and you come and applaud."

"Don't touch my embryo," Warren says.

16

Gray Water

MARVIN THE MOBILE MECHANIC IS POLISHING A GUN AND SAYS to Roxanne, "If you want life to go by fast."

"I don't want life to go by fast," Roxanne says.

"Build things," Marvin says. Then he twists on the stool. "If you can't build things fix things. You can convince yourself it's the same thing."

"Fixing is building?' Roxanne asks.

"It's not. It's the story you sell yourself. Then life goes by faster."

"How about cleaning?" she asks. "Cleaning is like fixing."

"Sure, it's a subset of fixing," he tells the gun barrel.

"You can fix things by cleaning them and that's like building," she says.

"Okay, cleaning is fixing and you can pretend it's building," he says.

"But life goes slow when I'm cleaning," she says and Marvin

says, "Well, you just haven't convinced yourself."

"Convinced myself what?" she asks.

"That cleaning is fixing is building," he says. "When I was in the war I got struck by a viper right here in the calf." He hikes up his workpants with the 38. "They tether snakes to poles then cover with sand or vegetation and you walk right over them, and they're already pissed off. I grabbed that snake in a death grip and squeezed until it was dead, and I walked around with that snake all day."

"I bet that day went slow," Roxanne says and I walk into the garage and ask, "What's going on here?"

"There's a snake in his fist," Roxanne explains.

"And a gun on the workbench," I say.

"I'm cleaning it," Marvin says.

"Hand it over," I say. "Handle first or whatever it's called. What are you doing scaring my girlfriend?"

"He's not scaring me," Roxanne says and I say, "Let's go to the cabin, Marvin," and in the cabin I say, "Time for a session," and he says, "So I finally got you mad."

"You are not getting this gun back," I say. "You can't just bring a gun here. So you want my attention. You got my attention."

"She's not your girlfriend," Marvin says. "Why do you call her your girlfriend? You're moving to Seattle."

"She is my girlfriend. She'll always be my girlfriend... when I look back," I say and he says, "This isn't therapy!" and I say, "So you're fixing my car for free. Why?" and he says, "So this is the moment is it?"

"Don't evade the moment by defining it," I say.

"But this is the moment, right?" he asks.

"Why are you fixing my car? What do you want out of it?" I ask.

"I want a hot chick to fall in love with me and I want to be admired," he says and slumps in his chair.

"What do you want to work on first, the hot chick or being admired?" I ask.

"The hot chick," Marvin says. "You believe any of this shit I'm handing you? Waiter, do you have frog legs? Then hop on over there and get me some chicken!"

"You know the thing about true love?" I ask.

"Here we go again. I'll bite. What?" he asks.

"It doesn't mean it works out. It just has staying power after the fact. So why don't you just get a new girlfriend?" I ask.

"All the chicks I know are druggies," he says

"Quod erat demonstrandum," I say.

"What?" he asks.

"It means ah-ha," I say.

"So why don't you say ah-ha?" he asks.

"I don't need a victory and you're looking for a trophy," I say. "I don't care if you quit drugs or admire yourself for doing it. But it makes scientific sense that both quitting drugs and admiring yourself would come before the hot chick who loves you. When you stop caring about something, there's a clarity that comes over you. I have that clarity now. So get lost and come back clean or don't come back at all. Quit drugs first, hot chick second. There's your moment. Admire yourself and others will admire you. Then along comes the hot chick."

"Gray water," Joe says, pointing at a pipe protruding from the rockery. "This one comes from the kitchen sink. There's another one coming from the downstairs shower. That's why the aloe looks so good out here. Toilets, mind you, go into your septic—in your case, small septic. Thing about gray water is it's best to scrape all the food off your plates before washing them in the sink. Otherwise you attract skunks and coyotes where it pours onto the land, and snakes too probably. But if you'd attached the gray water pipes to your small septic, the extra water would have drawn more roots up your French drains. So I say gray water is good."

I hand Joe the gun and say, "Maybe I *do* need a victory. Let me know if you see Marvin around. We had an argument and I think he's done here."

"You let him get to you," Roxanne says. "That hurt his feelings."

"He brought a gun here," I say and she says, "Here is your problem, the word here."

"Don't feel alone," Joe says. "It's the world's problem."

I stare at the dripping water from the pipe and it's not gray.

"Just a name they give it," Joe says and Roxanne says, "Now you have to go to his house and make up with him before he disappears."

"Take the gun," Joe says.

"He's coming back," Roxanne says and Marvin is walking up the middle of the road and turns in at the giant jades and takes long strides toward us.

"Nice gun," he says, grabbing it from Joe. "Looks like someone cleaned it."

"I have a gun too," I tell him, "After my divorce I lived between Bird Rock and Pacific Beach, you know where Loring dead-ends at the ocean?"

"Did it have southwestern exposure?" Marvin asks and sticks the gun in his belt.

"I took up rollerblading," I say.

"It's a good place for it," he says.

"Just skated and skated all day," I say. "Sometimes I'd listen to rush hour traffic reports just skating and skating on the boardwalk. The point is that I caught someone in my kitchen disconnecting my phone from the wall at three in the morning, and the guy ran when I rushed him and the cops said I was lucky because first they disconnect communications then they do what they do, so the next day I bought a gun. So I have one too, not that I ever clean it. I keep it hidden."

"Do you have diapers?" Joe asks.

"This is like road standing except its yard standing," Roxanne says. "We should go into the road."

"Or we can take the Avanti for a test drive," Marvin says.

"Do you mean right now?" Roxanne asks.

"That's all there is," Marvin says.

"You're really sucking up to him now," Roxanne says.

"Suck ups, apologies and guns, God Bless America," Marvin says.

"Diapers are good for cleaning guns," Joe says.

"Do you mean the Avanti is fixed?" Roxanne asks.

17

Embarcadero

I'M WITH SWIMS WITH HORSES AT THE EMBARCADERO AT THE waterfront in San Diego. I'm directing a film on mental illness for the hospital. I've taken a break and we're in a bar and Swims with Horses says, "Let's get out of here. The guy's a jerk."

The bartender she's referring to has been yapping his mouth off and talking loudly to a customer since he saw her. Every so often he glances over at our booth and I think to say, "The guy just doesn't know what to do with himself because of your beauty. You've seen it before," but I don't say it. I just store her swift judgment. "If you have a certain kind of long-boned beauty like yours, the world charges at you to entertain you, and I suppose you have to peel men away like cards if only to keep moving," but I don't say that either. We leave and I feel the bartender's eyes burning a hole in the back of her head. I do have a fleeting thought about when might I be the jerk she feels she has to peel away? The guy was just frozen by her cold beauty. But outside, the sun immediately feels right. I'm not a fan of swift judgments, but I'm also not a gorgeous woman.

She says, "I'm in trouble with his family again because his sister is pregnant and I made a comment about getting back to normal in a week."

"You know what talking shit is?" I ask.

"Of course," she says.

"It's making a conclusion about something you haven't experienced. You ought to avoid that around people instinctively leaning toward hating you," I say.

"Hating me?" she asks.

"For your beauty," I say and she says, "You are so sweet. I keep forgetting that about you because I focus on your intelligence. That's why I want you - for your mind. Women hate me."

"Women hate my wife, too," I say. "I once saw a guy come all the way across the dance floor to pull out a chair for her and I was sitting right there beside her. He got the look that kills from his wife when he walked back. Don't you want me for my body? I feel I've slipped sideways and down."

"Tonight is eggplant parmesan," she says. "I should go to the market while I'm here. Does your wife know she's hated by women?"

"You can cook?" I ask. "You can't expect the woman of your dreams to rise from your dreams and cook."

"You need to get me out of your dreams," she says.

"Oh, it's a dream," I mutter and roll over and she walks away in the crowd in her tank top and running shorts.

She turns at the Star of India all long arms and long legs and a face of humor and refinement, and I'm in my shirt and tie and white lab coat because I'm in the next scene, and she waves. We're in a Chinese restaurant and Swims with Horses wedges off one shoe and places her toes in my crotch. Long legs, I close my eyes.

"What you do?" Natasha asks and I mutter, "Something. Something wrong," and she says, "See I know how to wake a man. Rabbi on hotline says he wants to spin my dreidel," and the Native

America anthropologist puppy killer on the far side of her says, "Leave him alone because he's dreaming parakeets."

18

Tomatoes

THE AVANTI MOVES WITH THE SMOOTH ASSUREDNESS OF A WELL engineered heavy car. The feel that is only Avanti enters my hands as we pass Mary Jane Park and head onto the winding miracle that is La Cresta Road. The smell in the car is overpowering with Joe smelling of cats and nicotine and Marvin smelling of grease and BO.

La Cresta winds down the mountain, down alongside cacti, sumac, eucalyptus, orange, grapefruit and the bright red soil.

"Threw a rod right here," Marvin says, pointing out at the sumac and Roxanne says, "Another vote of confidence," and Joe says, "What is this thing we're in again?"

"Road-kill," Roxanne shouts and hits Marvin in the back of the head.

"What's that noise?" Joe asks.

"What's that smell?" Roxanne asks.

"What noise?" Marvin asks, shooing Roxanne off like she's a

buzzing fly.

"That's a grinding sound," Joe says.

"There's no grinding sound," Marvin says.

"It's from the brakes," Joe says.

"I didn't work on the brakes," Marvin says.

"Then why are they grinding? They should only be grinding if you worked on them," Joe says.

"They're not grinding. I worked on the steering," Marvin says.

"How's the steering?" Joe asks me.

"Road-kill," Roxanne shouts.

"Steering feels fine," I say and Joe says, "I always like looking at the beautiful homes they build down here against the cliffs."

"But he has the best place," Roxanne says.

"You do have a good place," Joe says and I take a right at the bottom of La Cresta onto Greenfield Drive.

Now we're driving along the bottom flat of the hole that is El Cajon.

"There it is!" Joe says.

"Tomatoes thirty-three cents!" Roxanne shouts and I pull left across oncoming traffic and swerve into a parking spot next to Maria's.

There is no sign outside to say Maria's. There isn't even a Maria. It's just a name Roxanne gives endlessly stacked fruit and vegetable boxes labeled Imperial Valley. Latinas and Latinos sidle around metal tarp-stanchions in that wandering working way. The place is small in the largest sense for small. It's a covered outside area and a wooden shack inside area that's never empty and is as much a roadside stand as the center of the universe.

"One of my favorite places," I say as Marvin dives under the front of the Avanti.

"Hey, Marvin, this is a celebration for you," Roxanne says. "That's why we're here. So get out from under the car."

"He's more comfortable under the car," Joe says and I ask, "So what's the verdict under there?"

"Looks good," Marvin says.

"Then get out," Joe says.

"Look at these," Roxanne says, calling out from across the street, holding up two casaba melons.

"Look at them melons," Marvin says, brushing off his pants.

"He's out," Joe says.

"What the hell is this place?" Marvin asks. He's looking around. Now he's with Joe staring into a bin.

"Christ!" Marvin says.

"I don't see Christ there," Joe says.

"Then you don't see him anywhere," Marvin says.

Roxanne smiles.

"Rotten bananas," Joe says.

Marvin holds up a handful and squeezes. Brown oozes squished through his greasy spatula fingers.

"You're out of control," Joe whispers.

"Go figure," Marvin says.

"People buy from this bin," Joes says.

"It's disgusting," Marvin says.

"It's a dime," Joe says.

"It shouldn't even be free. It's just rotted crap," Marvin says.

"Maybe someone will make a smoothie or banana bread out of it," Joe says.

"Maybe I'll die and go to heaven," Marvin says.

"Okay, Marvin, so it's a bad bin. I'll give you that," Joe says, stepping away.

"I feel victorious," Marvin says, dancing around with his arms in the air.

"The good stuff is in there," Joe tells him.

I pull Marvin to another outside bin and say, "I have to tell you something. It just came clear to me."

"What came clear to you," he asks and I say, "I found this place."

"So?"

"So, I found this place. I found maybe five other places like this."

"I don't get what you are saying," he says.

"I'll lay it out. I don't want to be too excited about this. But a person can't just find these places. A person can't even see these places unless his soul is healing," I say. "You have to find a state of grace to allow places like this to reveal themselves."

"I have to tell you something too," Marvin says. "Your steering fluid is still leaking."

"The steering fluid still leaks?" I ask.

"Not the point," he says. "How come I'm your patient and *you* talk about *your* healing?"

"Just find a few places like this," I tell him and he says, "I found one. Your place."

"My place?" I ask.

"I like your place," he says.

"That's nice," I say.

"Can I have your place?" he asks. "Since you're moving to Seattle?"

"Tomatoes," Roxanne calls from inside the shack.

There are no bins inside the shack. There are high boxes tilted for display.

"The best produce in the world," Roxanne says. "Look at these tomatoes. Have you ever seen jalapeño peppers this size? No dents, no pitting in them. Smooth as a green baby's bottom. Check out the cilantro. I *love* this place."

"Limes and we're done," Joe says, "salsa Crest style."

"Oh, no," Roxanne says. "Let's get all the fruit we can carry. I'll make a fruit salad and Sangria."

"You're so hot and smart," Marvin tells her and she puts her brown arm around his shoulder and says, "Thanks, Marvin."

"Remember, never pay more than thirty-three cents for tomatoes ever," she says. "It's the new standard for validity."

"Worth the trip. Let's go," Joe says.

But Marvin is saying to the Latina cashier who doesn't speak

English, "How many divers does it take to circumcise a whale? Four," he says. "Four skin-divers, four-skin divers, four skin divers, get it? Four *skin* divers. Four *divers*."

Joe grabs him by the scruff of the neck and pulls him away laughing and screaming. We all pile back into the car. I make a U-turn out of the parking space and head down the street.

Roxanne says, "I don't care if you *are* hooked on meth, you're the funniest man I know."

"He's hooked on meth?" Joes asks.

"It's because I've been stoned all the time," Marvin says.

"It will turn on you," I say.

"Mister, I think *I'll* turn on you to the cops," Joe says.

"You can't," I say.

"Why can't I?" Joe asks.

"There are two reasons," I say. "First is because without him I don't have a patient."

"Would you rather have a patient or a mechanic?" Joe asks.

"A mechanic," I say

"You want a mechanic who does meth?" Joe asks.

"No," I say.

"Then, you Mister," Joe says turning to Marvin, "there's *do* and there's *don't do*. Now you can don't do, see, or I'll call the cops. I'll drop a dime on you."

"I already quit today, so you're too late," Marvin says.

What's the other reason?" Joe asks.

"Me?" I ask.

"You said two reasons," Joe says.

"Big Larry needs someone to annoy him into talking more," I say. "Marvin annoys him more than anyone. It's a new job for Marvin. I've been thinking about it."

"You'll pay me to annoy Big Larry?" Marvin asks.

"Just be you," Joe says.

"I get to annoy him for money?" Marvin asks again.

"You're on the payroll," I say.

"This is a big day for me," Marvin tells Joe. "I stop *do*ing drugs and get paid to annoy someone. I am Veblen. I am Veblen."

"Empty your pockets," Roxanne tells him, "Empty them right here!"

"Hey get off me."

She's crawling all over him.

"Get off!" Marvin cries.

"I found a skin diver. What's this? What's this?" Roxanne yells.

"Don't ask me to ride in this car again," Joe says.

"How bad is the leak?" I ask.

"What leak?" Joe asks.

"He said it's leaking," I say.

"Can we make it home?" Joe asks.

"I said get off!" Marvin screams. "Hey, don't throw that out!"

"This will end badly," Joe says.

"What will?" I ask.

"This ride for instance," he says.

"Steering fluid," I say.

"That's what's leaking?" Joe asks.

"That's what he says," I say.

"Isn't that what he's been fixing?" Joe asks.

"Hey what are those cyclists doing hitchhiking?" Marvin asks.

"Oh, them, they always wait at the bottom of La Cresta and try to grab a ride off a guy's bumper," Joe says.

"That's how they get up the hill," Roxanne says.

"Up yours and the horse you rode in on!" Marvin shouts out the window, giving them the bird followed by the sideways bird.

"Who's Veblen?" Joe asks.

"Big Larry will be talking in no time," Roxanne says.

19

Transmission Towers

"THE OLYMPIC PENINSULA IS A DANGEROUS PLACE THAT makes you crazy," Warren says to the university faculty.

He shifts his position in the large van so he's facing directly back at them.

"People go insane here," he says. "They even go insane on the borders of here. Sometimes a whole community goes insane so there's no way to know *you're* insane. I've seen it. I've been it. This is wilderness. Tourists get killed out here. They arrive in Bermuda shorts and long white socks. Next thing you know, their names are on the news. Tides swirl in behind you when you're looking for razor clams. The last thing you see as you drown is your vehicle floating past, the one they won't find for weeks before they find your body."

With that, Warren extends the palm of his hand to the van doors and everyone in Julia's vision quest expedition up the Wynoochee shuffles out with backpack and sleeping bag. Its deep summer, heavy summer, the part of summer where things happen that stay with you for a lifetime.

Warren and the faculty begin descending a long, steep, dried waterfall of red rocks.

"Watch your step," he tells them, "better to have an injury at the end of the experience than at the beginning. You can't tell anyone about this place. This place is a secret. Okay?"

"Okay," everyone says and he waits for everyone to say it.

Way down at the bottom almost between our legs and the size of pencils we can see people moving and smoke rising. It seems impossible to climb down terrain so steep. Every rock must be grabbed and tested before weight is placed on it to the next rock. Watching the person beside you or below you gives a clue for possible routes. Perspective comes in close. Watch your own hand. Watch your own feet. Lay your body into the rocks. You're crawling down vertically. There are no instructions. You figure it out. This is grown-up stuff. I push outward like I'm doing a pushup and look up. Instead of sky, all I see is the cliff I've climbed down so far. It's straight above my head. I look down and I'm about halfway down the waterfall.

"See?" Natasha says next to me. "Phil McPherson is there and Frank Sid is there and a couple of the Port Angeles crowd."

"I can make them out now," I say.

"See the river?" she asks.

"We didn't see it from up top," I say.

"No, we not see it there," she says.

"Warren and Julia have found a good route," I say.

"Yes, we climb to that side," Natasha says. It's almost like we're yelling at each other though we're in touching distance. "Maybe people above follow us?"

Soon we're another quarter of the way down the rock face and Warren is already working with the Port Angeles crowd stacking wood in a large pile, mostly driftwood from the banks of the Wynoochee.

Julia is standing at the bottom of the rocks and she says to me, "Soon I return to school and you come be professor too."

"No," I say, taking my first step onto flat ground.

"You come give guest lecture then," she says.

"No," I say.

"He not interested," Natasha says.

"You now speak for him?" Julia asks then says, "Lots of university opportunity for networking here."

"Julia!" Warren shouts from the fire. "When everyone makes it down, bring them here."

Julia stares in his direction then turns back to us.

"He boss now," she says, "boss of the moment," and she helps the first faculty member off the waterfall.

At the campfire, Warren says to everyone, "Done before noon. That's a good job. Your lessons are your own in everything that happens here. Pay attention to your thoughts, not that you'll have a choice. We'll come back here. This is home base. Two of our Port Angeles friends will stay here to tend the fire. The rest walk with me." Then Phil McPherson hands each person a long-stemmed mushroom.

We're walking down the river which is ankle deep and knee deep in the holes and dry in the middle up on the sandbars, and the river is wide and has river sounds. We're following Tundra the grey ghost dog. We walk on the stones on the riverbank. We walk on the stones in the river. We walk like a human wall side-by-side, then in scattered patterns like cattle, then in a line. We climb the steep bank on the far side of the river. We duck under a bridge. Some people nibble on their mushrooms. Some just hold them. The girl next to Julia says, "I ate my whole mushroom." We walk on a hardened lava flow with rainwater stagnant and shiny as mirrors in the pockets. We stop there. Sit there. Mushrooms are eaten. A fallen old growth cedar descends a ravine four stories below us and ends on an island that splits the river.

"That's the spot," Warren says, pointing down there, but

nobody goes so he straddles the old growth cedar and edges his way down it. Nobody follows. He sidles his way back up and finds everyone grouped around a rain mirror. He says to me, "You do it. Maybe they'll follow you," but they don't.

I'm alone on the island at the bottom of the ravine. I must have slipped because I'm bleeding a bit from my chest and my arms. I look up to where everyone is supposed to be, but they're slightly around the bend now, so I don't see anything but the raging part of the river and the big rocks and the long old growth log above. I walk onto the island into the forest of the island, where I lay in the vegetation and lean back on my elbows, and there's Marvin the Mobile Mechanic.

I have to do a double take to make sure it's him.

"Old growth everywhere," he says. "Look up, way up. The tips of those giants belong more to the sky than the ground. It's like the Himalayas. Someone said that about the Himalayas. They belong more to the-"

"You can imagine my surprise," I tell him, "when we climbed down the dry red rock waterfall and there's Phil McPherson, Frank Sid and the Port Angeles crew inviting Julia's university types to a mushroom ceremony. Except it wasn't a ceremony. They just gave us each a big mushroom and we started walking downriver," and he says, "Well what did you think vision quest was?" and I say, "I figured we all would just sit in nature and think."

"Look at you," he says. "You're sitting in nature and thinking."

"Marvin, I'm sorry what happened to you," I say.

"What happened to me?" he asks.

"Maybe the best thing for me is I don't create any more realities for people to behave in," I say.

"Look," he says. "That's what you do. That's why you're here. You're trolling for clients."

"Not anymore," I say.

"Oh, sure you are," he says. "I know your technique. You try to help from the inside. So here you are looking for the thing that will find you. You taught me how to look for things like that."

"Like what?" I ask and he says, "Like that will find you."

"How do you look?" I ask.

"You don't look," he says. "What you do is you get yourself right. Then you become a vessel for the things that are looking for you. You're invisible to them until you get yourself right."

"What's get yourself right?" I ask.

"It's for its own sake. That's what right is," he says.

I roll over on the grass and every grass blade is like a tiny alien looking like a transmission tower. Each one is blinking and transmitting, and I ask Marvin, "Do you see this?" and he says, "Tiny aliens that look like a transmission towers?" and it's hard to breathe so I close my eyes and my wife asks, "Do you really think it's a good idea to bring him out here?"

"Sure, it'll be great this time. We have the money. We have the big house. The two of you can take the time getting your duo together again without worrying about money," I say and she says, "If you're so positive about it, Honey. It'll be nice to do something for my brother. I know they'll love California."

I walk into the living room and say to Marvin, "Now the house is a mess full of kids and musical instruments and amps and wires and cigarette smoke and cigarette butts. Just look at this. I can't stand to come home anymore," and he says, "That was the idea, right, because you're in love with Swims with Horses and she's in love with you. So you made up this reality for your wife so she could get her music career up and running again so she wouldn't miss you when you leave her. That's not so bad. You tried to help her, you cheater. Oh, I get it. This is an example of why you don't create any more realities for people to behave in. This is one of those realities."

"It is," I say.

"Then you should lie on that couch because you're *my* patient," he says. "How does it feel? You've always been my patient."

"This is so damn heavy," I say.

"Heavier than what happens to me whatever that was?" he asks.

"I hired you to help Big Larry," I say and he holds his hand open to my face and says, "Want to see my tattoo?"

"Who do you talk to?" Natasha asks.

"What?" I ask

"I find you. I come down log. Who do you talk to?" she asks.

I point into the raging river.

"Those boulders are alive," I say. "I must be talking to them. Everything is alive. I know that now. Even rocks are alive, especially rocks. They're very old, very strong and they're not happy with us. They're stern and knowing. They've seen everything from right here in the universal consciousness. Look at their faces."

"You come with me to others," she says and helps me up. It's a real hand, a warm hand, touching the way a human hand touches, and I feel I'm rising.

"Wobbly," I say, looking down at myself. "But it's good to stand."

"People ask for you but nobody sees you so I follow here," she says.

"That's nice of you," I say.

"I not eat the mushroom. Why you eat it again? What if I not find you?" she says.

"I would make it back," I say. "I know that about myself. It's the main thing I know. I would make it back."

"Maybe we climb up log now? That's a dangerous log. You fall and you die," she says.

She's holding my hand.

"Yes. I'll follow," I say.

"Yes, better you follow," she says.

"I'm a good follower," I tell her. "That's how I lead. I lead from behind. But this time I'll follow for real."

We are sidling up the log above the raging part of the river. My full attention is on keeping my balance by focusing on the back of Natasha's blouse. I force myself to keep remembering that her back is everything to me. It moves. I move. The river is four stories below now. I can hear it. I look down and see the angry faces on the rocks and the water surging. I've forgotten about her blouse at the moment she pulls me off the log and onto the lava and we crawl away from the log and she doesn't help me to my feet as we get around the corner but yells, "I find him!"

Julia and the university vision questers are staring into a lava reflection pool.

Everyone looks up and Frank Sid works in stages to get to his feet. First he's on his knees. Then he sticks his butt in the air. Then he walks his hands toward his feet in a jackknife and rises. I think he's coming to help me up, but instead he pulls off all his clothes and yells, "I want to spawn and die!" and he runs upriver.

"We go now," Natasha says and yanks Julia under her armpits, once, twice, three times. Now Julia is on her feet. The rest of the group rises like dust then begins walking upriver ahead of us rickety-like and unevenly then just slowly. Natasha seems to herd them. She guides laggers inward. The banks grow steep on each side. A tiny bird splashes in the spray of the stream then flies off having taken a shower. The group approaches the bridge and has to climb up the side, across the road then down the other side, where the river suddenly flattens to a delta. Tundra the grey ghost dog appears walking along the bank then tiptoeing on the river stones. Now she's splash-walking the river. Between us and Tundra, the faculty vision questers march in scattered patterns like cattle in a flooded field. Then they are in a line walking with Tundra toward the fire.

"It feels good," I say to Natasha.

"What does?" she asks.

"To walk with you," I say.

"Look, feel your path you come so far," she says and I say, "My balance is getting better," and she says, "It's so much fun to feel balance," and I say, "It is."

Heads are counted around the fire. Warren is missing. Phil

McPherson is missing. Naked Frank Sid is missing. Dusk arrives with mosquitoes. The fire is built higher. Sparks fly to the river, and there's Frank Sid wrapped in a blanket and being led across the river by Warren and Phil McPherson.

Warren sits and says, "Found him walking along the logging road and had to push him into the bushes when the Forest Ranger's truck went by."

"And another fine disaster avoided," Phil McPherson says, taking out his drum and rattle from a pillow case.

"I don't see a talking stick," I whisper hopefully to Natasha.

"Can't avoid," she says and the drumming begins.

It brings on full darkness so suddenly it's like a striker to a stretched elk skin - boom, dark - and with darkness comes the smell of salmon. Frank Sid has placed several planks of salmon upright in wire contraptions against the fire. Everyone around the fire is visible in light spasms, sitting up wrapped in a sleeping bag or blanket, like little light spasm faces peering out of caves.

I whisper to Natasha, "I'll toss the talking stick for Tundra."

"Shush," she whispers.

"I will," I say.

Phil McPherson is now singing pseudo-Indian hip-hop to his drum accompaniment.

He sings, "Vision quest Spirit hey-anna-he-nay-hey-yana-na, we thank you for yana-he-nay, our insight and return. We thank you, forest flowers, for giving us safe space. Thank you, thank you for he-nay awakening and your yana wisdom to allow us to live within your consciousness these milliseconds hey-ana-he-nay-hey-yana-na with our new friends from the un-i-ve-rsi-ty."

The forest ranger shows up in my mind shouting, "What the fuck is this!" and it makes me laugh.

Julia gives me the elbow.

Natasha repeats, "Shush!" and Frank Sid passes sticks of salmon in both directions without looking up from the fire. Greasy mouths and greasy fingers appear in light spasms.

Warren says to me, "Man, how many times did you climb up and down that log trying to get us to follow you? It must have been ten times."

"Yeah, did you see this guy?' one of the spasms asks.

"I don't remember doing that more than two times," I whisper to Julia and one of the faculty members says, "Didn't you hear us chanting don't fall off the log, don't fall off the log?" and a couple of the greasy spasms chant, "Don't fall off the log, don't fall off the log!"

"Is this what this is? We all get unhinged?" I ask.

"You've been unhinged before," a light spasm says.

"I spend my life unhinged," I say, and, when his face flints again, he's smiling and the talking stick is in his hand.

"I'm chair of the Anthropology Department," he says.

"This is going to be a long talking stick," I whisper and Marvin says, "You mean the complaining stick?" and Julia pokes me and the chair says, "Barry, my name is Barry," and I understand he's introducing himself. "I am grateful for this internal and external journey you've taken us on. Thank you, Julia, for introducing us to your friends. I hand the talking stick to Warren."

"God almighty, where's the plaque?" Marvin sighs.

Warren says, "I'm Warren. Some of you think I'm over-chicked." He pats Julia's knee. "She's pregnant with my baby."

"I not pregnant!" Julia shouts and grabs the talking stick. "You not over-chicked. You no-chicked," and she gives me the talking stick and Phil McPherson is drumming hard and the chair is flicker-staring me down and Marvin says, "It's so fucked up everyone is so fucked up. The only person who isn't fucked up is the one who's really fucked up and that's Big Larry. Lost the use of half his body and never lost his sense of humor, how fucked up is that? It's what that guy told us about Jesus being the fat lady on the bus but we walk past because she's the fat lady on the bus and we're just all fucked up because everyone is except Big Larry because he really is. Like George Orwell said. Who controls the past controls the future. Who controls the present controls the past. The past is an invention of those controlling the present in order to control the future."

"Where *that* come from?" Julia asks and I realize I said it.

Bright stars, deeper night, only the crackling fire breaks the silence of the circle.

"A good friend of mine, my last patient," I am saying, staring at the talking stick. "He's been explaining to me that my techniques could be faulty and spilling over into my life. I've been creating realities for people. They have behaviors inside those realities. Those behaviors surface cures for them. But realities once established set unforeseen machinery in motion. I did that to my ex-wife when I was leaving her. So godammit are you done explaining yourself?" Marvin shouts.

The next morning Julia, Natasha and I are climbing the dry red rock waterfall. We're not yet high enough to see the large van, but the faculty has disappeared over the top, and, below, the Port Angeles crew moves up slowly. It's steep and tough going. Julia says, "Chair Barry like you so much. He told me he got a lot out of you and your cure behaviors lecture. He says maybe you join faculty?"

"He not interested," Natasha says and Julia says, "I break up with Warren again so no more Indian me. Summer gone soon school."

Natasha turns to me.

"See how simple is brutality," she says as she steps up to the next rock.

"We Russian not Ojibwa," Julia tells her. "But Warren smart. He tell me plant medicine just drugs, that why Port Angeles friends do so many ceremonies like equinox-this equinox-that, full-moon this part-moon that, birthday-this anniversary-that, reason-this reason-that, all for drugs so many ceremonies. But he says can make money too from searchers think they so smart. Watch in van he sell abalone shells and turkey feathers. Maybe *Warren* do guest lecture?"

20

Zamboners

LORING REACHES A DEAD END AT THE OCEAN WHERE A HANDFUL of palm trees surround my previous home with the waves lapping the buttresses. "Looks like a castle," Roxanne says, putting on her rollerblades.

"I lived here for a year after my divorce and never made love in that place, but this is where I caught that guy in my kitchen at two in the morning unplugging my phone and that's why I bought the gun," I say.

"The one you don't know how to clean?" she asks.

"Yes," I say.

"We can break in now and make love," she says. "Hebrews eleven one, now faith is the substance of things hoped for, the evidence of things not seen."

I stand on my rollerblades, look at the house and beyond to the ocean and the surfers and say, "You want to talk about faith in something? I'd lace up my rollerblades every morning and skate on the streets all the way to the boardwalk then miles down to the rollercoaster way down there, see, then on down to the south parking lot then all the way back and back and back. Some days I'd keep skating until dark. Look!" I shout and a dolphin leaps north then leaps again.

"I see it," she says.

"It's a dolphin day," I tell her. "It's rare. It's a very rare day. You almost never see a dolphin, not in months, but when you do it's a dolphin day and that's special. No matter what you do that day, it's a dolphin day and today is a dolphin day."

"That's what we're going to do now, right? Skate all the way down to the south parking lot?" she asks and we skate up the middle of Loring. It's steep so we have to skate hard in a running manner and I shout, "Point your toes outward. Always make a platform of your lower leg and leap forward off it, left and right, left and right, up the middle of the road."

"You did great," I say. "It gets really crazy if there's traffic coming down. People get mad and there's no way out once you commit. But now it gets tricky. We have to skate down to the right and it's steep. We have to skate down the middle of the street. You have to watch for cars coming out of their driveways."

"I have faith," Roxanne says.

"Why?" I ask and she says, "Because it's a dolphin day."

"Use your brake," I say and she asks, "Where's yours?"

"I took them off," I say.

"Why?" she asks and I say, "Because I used to play roller hockey and you just can't have skates with brakes on them if you play roller hockey. You'd get laughed out of the arena. That's a part of my Pacific Beach story. An entire lifetime happened here."

I point south down the ocean.

"I'm a ghost here. *Lots* of my friends are. We're part of the forever reality of Pacific Beach. Every moment that I was here was like an out-of-body experience. Living on the ocean, skating up and down that boardwalk with my hockey stick, getting surprised by a dolphin day, it always surprises, a dolphin day, all just an out-of-body experience. I got well here."

We've started down the steep part of the street, twisting back and forth like on skis. Halfway down I stop to see how Roxanne is doing and she shoots past heading uncontrollably for the boardwalk. She hits the boardwalk with a shout and arms flailing. Then she starts coasting. When I catch up to her she's laughing.

"What was the name of your roller hockey team?" she asks.

"The Zamboners," I tell her and she collapses in a fit of hysteria.

I stand over her and a couple of skaters stop to see if she's okay, but she can't stop laughing and it looks like crying.

When she finally gets up she wipes her eyes and announces, "His roller hockey team was called the Zamboners," and the skaters skate away from us down the boardwalk, which isn't a boardwalk. Its smooth rolled cement with wooden cottages on the east side and a waist-high cement barrier on the west side keeping skaters from the beach and the ocean.

"I've seen skaters lose it and fly head over heels over that," I say as we skate south. "You know how I joined the team? I had a Toyota SR 5 with a liftback that wouldn't stay up so I had a hockey stick to keep the liftback up. I was parked in the south parking lot."

"Where we're going," she says.

"Yes, and these guys were playing roller hockey, so I decided to join in with the stick I used to keep the liftback up, and it turned out I was much better than they were, so the next thing I know I'm in a men's league and get approached by the upper division Zamboners."

"Oh, I'm having trouble controlling myself now!" Roxanne chokes and I have to hold her up as we skate.

"It gets better," I tell her and she chokes, "Oh, God, no!"

"Oh yes," I say. "The Zamboners, I'll tell you what it was like. I had a patient in Vista who was an accomplished graphic designer just ask him, you know one of those types?"

"One of what types?" she asks.

"Speaking like a therapist I'd say one of those means permanently stuck in Maslow's self-esteem phase, a self-involved type. He owned a house on what was once a poultry ranch so there were lots of rattlesnakes around. You always had to watch your step getting out of your car. He caught one and placed it in a terrarium and made a painting of it. You had to hear him. He said he spent months doing nothing but staring at that snake and getting to know every scale on its body. I'm sure that was true but it wasn't a good painting. Some people just get too close to the subject matter. That's how it was with roller hockey."

'Why wasn't it a good painting?" she asks.

"But that's not my point," I say.

"But why wasn't it?" she asks.

"It didn't look like a rattlesnake," I say. "It looked like component parts of a rattlesnake. The rattlesnake had–"

"No soul?" Roxanne offers.

"Yes, the speed, the strength, the danger–"

"Like your Zamboners?"

"No," I say. "I mean you can live inside a metaphor that doesn't extrapolate out."

"Out into what?" she asks.

"Reality comes to mind," I say.

"So the Zamboners weren't real?" she asks and I say, "All too not real. I mean we were in an extremely concentrated unreality."

"Oh that sounds like fun," she says. "What's that up there?"

In the wavy heat distance is the rollercoaster.

"See that?" I say pointing. "The Zamboners were sponsored by the owners of that rollercoaster. Remember the old Harry O TV show with David Jansen? The beginning sequence was shot there."

"The Harry show?" she asks and just then the boardwalk opens to the rollercoaster and its mall of restaurants and clothing stores. A girl in a thong leaps off the barrier and skates in front of us. Roxanne starts to giggle.

"See?" I tell her. "This place is an out-of-body experience. It's all like a movie."

"Nice butt," Roxanne says as we pass.

CUT TO: The Zamboners' dressing room which is no dressing room at all but the side of the boards at the roller rink in Chula Vista, a dingy stink hole with bad lighting. It's the championship game, the Zamboners against some league winner from Los Angeles and I'm late so I have to dress in front of the crowd comprised of four guys' girlfriends. I strip down to my underwear to pull on my cup and just then the owner's son, a skinny eighteen-year-old runt with dermatological issues, shows up with his girlfriend and starts yelling at me to get in the bathroom where nobody ever changes because it stinks. I tell him so. He shouts, "You can't play. Get out of here."

I tell Roxanne, "I pull up my cup then step into my hockey pants adjusting the pads and tightening the Velcro. The owner's son is screaming I'm calling the police to have you arrested for indecent exposure. So I look at his girlfriend and she's a normal, nice girl, and by now the Zamboners who have been skating through the warm-up drill pour over the boards and get between me and them."

CUT TO: The owner's son shouts, "He dropped his pants in front of my girlfriend!" and Randy, my left-winger, shouts, "Hey, I would, too! Watch," and he pulls up his Zamboner jersey to get at his suspenders. I reach into the crowd and roll him back toward me until I can whisper, "Not helpful."

"Well fuck him the little geek!" Randy shouts at the top of his lungs.

"Yeah, tell daddy to get us some real dressing rooms before you start showing your girlfriend what a big dick you've got!" Claude the right-winger shouts.

"Go suck your daddy's cock, you little cocksucker!" Sam shouts.

Sam is our extremely buff, Harley-riding defenseman who has the most penalty minutes in the league and he plays mad, starts mad, ends mad and wants to be an enforcer in the NHL. He lives somewhere in PB and I've seen him a few times on the boardwalk always with a different gorgeous woman. He throws a punch at the owner's son but only manages to hit the back of Pete's head, a square block of a guy who's an engineer at General Dynamics. So of course Pete turns around and goes after Sam and suddenly everyone is piling on everyone else.

Meanwhile our captain Joey who's about six foot six and an ER surgeon at Mercy has his arm around the owner's son's neck and is moving him a few feet toward the glass display case with all the dusty trophies and Joey leans down into him for a chat. Then all of a sudden the metal edge of someone's knee brace catches me in the eye. It must have been Pete because he had ACL surgery last year.

"Hey, shouldn't you be fighting *us*?" one of the L.A. guys calls from the rink. They're all just standing there on the other side of the boards watching us, and Sam shakes free of the pile and shouts, "Soon enough, assholes!"

A minute or two later the Zamboners are all on their feet readjusting their equipment and Joey skates over to me and says, "You'll have to apologize to this kid if you want to play."

"I'm already injured. I can't see out of my eye," I say and he says, "And your point is?" so everyone shuts up and I say, "I'm sorry. I should have changed in the bathroom. I apologize," and Sam shouts, "You fuckin' woos!"

"Can I play now?" I ask and the boss's son is holding his girlfriend's hand and says, "Okay but don't do it again," and the Zamboners get absolutely creamed by the L.A. team and lose the championship five to two.

"The first thing that happens is Sam spots a guy Number Twelve on the L.A. team who can barely skate and isn't near the skill level of the rest of us and this makes him angry," I tell Roxanne. "The far side of the Chula Vista roller rink is nothing but a high brick wall. Sam crushes Number Twelve into the wall for his first penalty. We're down a guy almost the whole game and that guy is Sam until he gets ejected from the game. He plays mad, starts mad and ends mad and soon leaves with one of his gorgeous women, yanking her out the door where he waits in the parking lot for Number Twelve."

Roxanne is laughing her head off as we skate toward the south parking lot.

"You lied to me!" she cries. "You said you weren't a fan of team sports."

"I'm not," I say.

"Zamboner!" she cries.

"The place was a toilet holster," I say and she laughs, "A toilet holster?"

"A dive, a bad place, a rundown facility, you know, a toilet holster, and we played in lots of toilet holsters," I tell her. "We even played in a place that had a mirror ball because it was for dancing on roller skates. The wildest part was where the Zamboners practiced. Randy worked in the La Jolla Gateway complex as a CPA, so we'd show up in the underground parking structure of his building at eight at night. We'd set up our goals and play until seven in the morning because we had no conception of time. We'd just keep pounding each other into the concrete pillars and rushing back and forth scoring until suddenly some guy in a suit would drive down to our level in the garage and we'd realize it was morning and he was arriving at work and we got the hell out of there. We'd just grab our stuff and skate up to ground level then into the street. It was so much crazy fun because it all seemed so normal and everything else seemed so abnormal like that guy showing up in his suit. The friends you made there were just for there because that's where we really explained ourselves to ourselves so outside that was just a pale imitation. When we met on the street or in a restaurant it would just be yeah hi-how-you-doing and here is where it all started in this parking lot right here because I happened to have a hockey stick in my car to hold up my liftback."

"This is the most you ever talked to me," Roxanne giggles as she skates around the parking lot. I follow. It's another magical day in San Diego. The rock jetty beyond the parking lot splashes waves into the sky. The basketball court is empty. Sailboats move in their own dream. Grass meets sand and sand meets rock and rock meets water. There are almost never cars at this end of the boardwalk. There are none now. Roxanne is gorgeous. I tell her so. I say, "You are the perfect woman. Your legs don't even touch each other all the way up."

"Is that why I'm the perfect woman to you?" she laughs and we just keep skating around the parking lot.

I say, "Never ask an ER surgeon what's the strangest thing you ever saw. That's what I asked Joey after one game. You know what he said?"

"What? And I'm not sure I want to hear it," she says.

"He said just that week a sergeant from Camp Pendleton brought his wife in with their German shepherd attached to her. He said he had to give the dog a tranquilizer to get him to relax his penis. The Marine came home and found his wife on all fours on the kitchen floor with their dog stuck to her. He brought his wife into emergency with a blanket over her back. The Marine was pissed off too and his wife's back was all scratched up."

Roxanne asks, "What would you do if you came home and found me attached to a dog?" and I say, "All that dating, all those meals, and here's this dog who doesn't even have a credit card."

"I feel sorry for that girl," Roxanne says. "It must have been terrifying for her to wait for the dog to unlock and wonder if she'd get caught. That reminds me I had to buy a girlfriend a wedding gift so I went to one of those Love Shops. You know what I found?" She starts to giggle. "I found a Chia Dick."

"You mean the thing you rub seeds on and it grows into a plant?" I ask.

"Except this was a ceramic dick with balls," she says.

"Did you buy it?" I ask.

"I was laughing so hard the guy asked me to leave," she says.

We climb on the jetty and sit staring at the water. I ask, "When I say one-two-three, one-two-three what does it mean?"

"I don't know," she says.

"One-two-three, one-two-three," I say.

"I really don't know," she says.

"One-two-three then another one-two-three, it's the kick in the crawl. Shoulder-elbow-reach-pull, don't you get it?" I ask. "Didn't a swimming instructor ever teach you how to swim? That's what I studied. How clumps of information get lodged into the brain with their own entry points. Then internal codes access our secret language through synaptic gates to the infinitesimal points of our lives. But you only get to them in your own private re-showing. And you're the only one in the theatre except the people on the screen invited you in."

"What are you talking about?" she asks.

CUT TO learning how to swim at summer camp. It's cold in the lake. Seven of us are in the water holding on to the dock, and Mike in his McGill jacket and red bathing suit is standing over us, yelling, "One-two-three!"

CUT TO Christmas Day watching the ocean from inside the castle with no one on the beach but a girl dancing one-two-three in a red dress.

CUT TO staring at the thong of the girl skating in front of us again.

CUT TO the Over the Line tournament with the hairy ass guy in a thong and brown stains on his chest from sweating out Pepsi.

CUT TO Marvin the Mobile Mechanic shouting, "History of the World Part Two!" after he crushes his finger on the rusty brake cylinder.

Roxanne asks, "What's History of the World Part Two?"

"Something Marvin made up to access his memories, his clumps and synaptic gates," I say and she laughs, "You really are a Zamboner," and she climbs off the jetty to the parking lot and skates across it toward the boardwalk.

When I catch up to her I say, "Anyway this is where I got well."

"Got well from what?" she asks and I say, "True love gone

terribly wrong right before my eyes, an extremely concentrated unreality."

"Like the Zamboners," she says.

"Exactly my point," I say. "It took the Zamboners for me to see it. You know, through my clumps and synaptic connections, the things I started studying here. So that's how I got well here by rollerblading, crazy right?"

"I love it," she says.

"That's why you're the perfect woman," I say.

"Not because my legs don't touch?" she asks.

"Yes, actually, that's really why," I say and she asks, "Is that your house way up there?" and it is. I can see it like a watermark through the heat haze miles north at the Bird Rock hook on the ocean.

"How come you lost the game?" she asks.

"We were too good for them and we got behind and it made us crazy because we were insulted to be even playing against them in the first place," I say. "Then Sam got kicked out of the game, but the real reason was because they left a cherry picker down beside our goalie the whole game. This guy just stayed down by our net no matter where the puck was, and anytime they got the puck they just iced it to this cherry picker. Sometimes he scored and sometimes he didn't. It was bad sportsmanship. We really should have quit but we played the whole game and then the team just broke up and we never played another game. It was as if a germ had been placed inside us. So we lost because we were too good for anyone to play fairly against us."

"Were you always rich?" she asks and I say, "No. I wasn't even always smart."

"But you're smart now," she says.

"I remind myself about something. I say to myself don't act like an orphan," I say. "Act like part of a community. At least act like you have a team."

"Oh, look," she says. "We've made it back to the rollercoaster."

I say, "That's what I'm working on with Marvin, expunging the permanent record."

"Like you did for yourself?" she asks.

"Yes," I say. "You know what memory is, all which has come and gone. Gone is the operative word. But then along comes the worm experiment. Chop up a worm and feed it to another worm and the second worm has the memories of the worm it ate."

"What memory does a worm have?" she asks.

"For one thing how to negotiate a maze," I say. "That's a fairly valuable memory to have. So even if you chop yourself up and feed yourself to yourself, you still have those memories."

"But the first chopping kills you, right?' she asks. "But what might we expect from a Zamboner?"

"Incremental awareness," I say.

"I know who you are," Roxanne says, and we've finally skated off the boardwalk and to the top of Loring. "You're the Zamboners' therapist."

"I am!" I say.

"So what's the cure, Doctor?" she asks.

"Movement," I say. "I found I could skate fast enough into stillness. Then everything takes care of itself and I found you."

"Oh, so sweet," she says. "Race me down to the house. We can break in and make love. *I'll* show you movement."

"I'll show you stillness," I say.

"Then truth arrives," she says

"Maybe a cop arrives?" I say.

"Come on, it's a dolphin day. What can happen?" she asks.

"And there it is, Your Honor, the question whose answer is in doubt," I say.

"You know how to get in don't you?" she asks. "It was your house, your home, what did you call it, the castle? I want this for you. I want to do this. Eat your own chopped worm and you would have been here and made love."

We're at the back door ringing the bell but no one is home and the key is under the red tile. We go in and Roxanne whispers,

"Don't make me do it fast just because you want to get out of here," and a woman's voice from upstairs yells, "Who's there?"

21

Big Larry Returns

THE SUN GENTLY MOVES OVER CREST LIKE A GIANT BEACH BALL rolling between the eucalyptuses. Then it smashes into the open and cracks down on El Cajon. And as El Cajon fries like oil, gentle light fingers stream back through the leaves up on Crest and across the Avanti on cinder blocks in Big Larry's driveway. The hood is open and one of Big Larry's peacocks is on the roof. The peacock makes a scratching gesture at the paint and cries, "Ma, ma, ma." Marvin's puppy, Buster, lying by a pile of tires, snaps at a dragonfly. Broken glass is nearby with light glinting off the edges and broken pots have flowers popping up in them. Chickens are everywhere dancing to J.J. Cale booming from the outdoor speakers, "Magnolia, you sweet thing. You're driving me mad. Got to get back to you, babe. You're the best I ever had. You're the best I ever had."

I can see Marvin's legs jutting out from under the car and part of Big Larry's wheelchair.

Roxanne is over there laughing and telling them, "It's me the guy who sold you the house. It's a dolphin day so I have to make love to my girlfriend right here if that's okay?"

"Good thing you didn't get shot," Joe says to me.

"She gave us a bedroom," I tell him and he shakes his head and says, "All the life seems to be next door now. What's Larry doing *now*?"

Big Larry gets out of his wheelchair and starts walking with his canes toward the street. He disappears behind the giant entry jades and emerges moving ever so slowly up my driveway. When he finally gets to us, and it takes forever, he whispers out of breath, "Pre-ve-ventive maintenance for l-l-long term ownership. History of the World Part Two," then he turns and walks back down the driveway onto the street then up his own driveway, where he flops exhausted in his wheelchair.

"It's been like this for weeks, always the same," I say to Joe. "Marvin sends Big Larry to me with a meaningless message. Yesterday was better. It was the reason the invisible hand seems invisible is because it is not there."

"Can I take the Ford Ranger?" I call to Roxanne and she waves yes with a smile.

"Where are you going?" Joe asks and I say, "To take my life in my hands."

"What does that mean?" he asks and I say, "Visiting my old hospital."

"I'll fix that faucet while you're gone," he says.

Twenty minutes later I walk through the Emergency doors at Mercy Hospital. Old habits die hard. I never entered the front way. I wander the corridors and find myself in the cafeteria, where I see my former colleague Dorothy Charles, redhead, sensible shoes, nasal, tight body, brilliant doctor, buying a bagel.

Never ever expected to see *you* again," she says. "Come join me. I'll sit over there."

"I'll get an ice tea," I say.

When I join her, she says, "I miss the East - the sarcasm and the brick. What was that thing Louis Kahn said about the sun never knew how beautiful it was until it hit the side of a building? It's busy today. On hot weekends, people drink and fall on sharp objects in their backyards."

I sip the ice tea. It is a hot day. I just realize it.

"What are you doing here? Rumor has it you were dead," she says. "You're a sight for sore eyes, though, if you ask me. We all saw the dive you took when your marriage and affair fell apart at the same time, your addiction or whatever. All that respect you lost around here, we all saw you lose her. She came back last year for a visit. After she left everyone wanted to know who she was. You know how she looks and speaks. There's an expression in night sailing about one hand for yourself and one hand for what you're doing. The one hand for yourself is the hand that's always holding something so you don't get swept overboard. Who ever thought you'd forget about that one hand for yourself? What are you doing now? You lost your practice. You lost your equilibrium, your car keys and your pride. That's Tom Waits, remember? Do you at least still have your video company? What's the name of it, Medical Video Productions? You were the therapist turned movie producer. Nice gig. What are you wearing?"

"They're called jeans," I say.

"I only ever saw you in a suit and a lab coat," she says.

"I live in Crest on a small acreage. It seems like I'm always trying to repair something. Jeans make sense doing physical labor. Do you know where Crest is?" I ask.

"It's above El Cajon," she says and I say, "I have a small practice and a girlfriend." I look around the cafeteria. "Thank God you're the only one I bumped into here."

"Don't be relieved. You never know who might walk through those doors," she says. "Why are you here?"

"I have a patient. I want to get a consult," I say.

"I can do that for you," she says.

"I don't need a psychiatrist. I need a neurologist, a consult on the operation for nicking the trigeminal nerve," I say.

"But still you have to admit it's a good test for you to walk in here. Tell me about your girlfriend," she says.

"She's the nicest person," I begin to say and Dorothy Charles says, "Doesn't sound like your type?"

"She laughs a lot. Giggles actually," I say.

"Everyone laughed around you. At least they used to," she says.

"I have a patient like that. His name is Marvin the Mobile Mechanic. That's his full name. Ask me what he does," I say.

"Is that funny or meant to be funny?" she asks.

"He's a jokester. You know they have thick walls, jokesters. I found a therapy for him. I guess it's a therapy. I deflected him to the one person who won't put up with his smokescreen. I told him to lay the smokescreen on thick because that's the only thing that will help this other person. I think they're both going to take each other apart. The other person is also a patient of mine, a secret patient. He doesn't know he's a patient."

"Does Marvin know he's your patient? What's Marvin's therapy?" she asks.

"To fix the unfixable car and also to fix this other patient who needs a tremendous amount of stimuli," I say. "Roxanne is looking over both of them. She doesn't know she's doing it. I tried to explain what I'm doing but she's a layperson."

"What do you mean?" Dorothy Charles asks.

"You know what I mean. Do you explain theory to your husband? Of course you don't," I tell her. "You're just getting it out loud for yourself. She confuses good and well. Intuitively she gets everything. She did something for Marvin that was outstanding. I think it was the best thing."

"Her name is Roxanne? That's a nice name. But she's not a therapist? You should always date a therapist. But even then not everyone is an equal," she says. "Have you considered that you're playing below your level?"

"I don't feel that way. I'm moving to Seattle. I told Roxanne because of her I can finally leave because she brought me whole with this place," I say.

"So she's losing you?" she asks.

"I don't know about losing," I say. "But it's funny you say playing below my level because there's an expression in hockey that the only time you really get hurt is when you play below your level. Amateur players swing their sticks to catch their balance and make moves you'd never expect from someone who knows what he's doing."

"Do you know what you looked like near the end?" she asks and I say, "I have inside knowledge about that."

"What was the lesson?" Dorothy Charles asks.

"When it's set up as wrong, nothing you do will be right. Murphy's Law, the third tenet, nature sides with the hidden flaw," I say.

"And she's in Seattle, right?" she asks and I say, "Maybe I'll get out the back end of Seattle?"

"But you're not there yet," she says. "You're not at the place you need to get out the back end of. But you're still heading in the direction of the one person on earth who chewed you up. Remember this. The abused child always runs to the abuser. I have a sister in Seattle who runs a private hospital and probably needs a video or a staff therapist. I'm sure she does. Here's her number in case you end up pushing a shopping cart through Pioneer Square."

"It sounds unhealthy brought out loud. I'll give you that," I say and Dorothy Charles says, "There is also a reality where things brought out loud sound healthy."

"I am healthy," I insist.

Dorothy Charles leans forward and asks, "Will you let her know you're there?"

"I just need to get under the same sky," I say.

"For what?" she asks.

"For truth," I say.

"Fine, here's the summary," she says. "You say you're only

leaving because things are so good. I say stay and build on what *is* so good. *That's* healthy."

"This place has too many ghosts," I say.

"They'll follow you," she says and all the while she is gorgeous, so I say, "And all the while you are gorgeous."

"You always were sweet until you lost it," she says.

"I'm sweet again," I tell her.

"Then congratulations on your recovery and impending reversal," she says.

"You're the only one who knows all this about me. How does it feel?" I ask.

"Like another day at work," she says and I say, "I've finally done well here. I can do well there."

"You mean do good don't you?" she asks. "You make peace then move the battlefield. Warrior mentality is an addictive trait. I'm just mentioning it for your consideration. So what are you doing this afternoon? Are you driving back to Crest to screw your sweet girlfriend before you dump her by making it her idea? Or does she already know to make it her idea?"

"Actually I thought I'd stick around the rest of the afternoon and apply for your job," I tell her and she says, "We remember your therapy here. There's a new war now and we need you. Beauty is as beauty does. Actions speak louder than words. Walk the walk don't talk the talk. Character is destiny. Young overachievers turned gung ho murderers. The brighter the light the darker the shadow it casts. That was you, right?"

"There was a helicopter pilot. He was flying some soldiers behind the lines. They had two prisoners and wanted information. They asked the first who said nothing so they threw him out at eight hundred feet. The second talked immediately," I say.

"What did they do with him?" she asks.

"They threw him out too. Combat vets carry a lot," I say.

"If she spoke to you in Seattle would a kind word be enough for you?" she asks.

"Yes," I say.

"You're looking for God to speak to you," she says.

"I didn't come to get beaten up if this is your new therapeutic approach," I say.

"I'm your friend," she says.

"I've had friends like you. I was able to get away from them. I wasn't sure that I could, but I did. I got away," I said.

"So why did you come back?" she asks.

"I was having a particularly good day. Everything was going well for people I care about. It was almost a dolphin day if you must know. So I chanced fate and fate delivered you," I say.

"Delivered me as what?" she asks.

"Proof," I say.

"Proof of what?" she asks.

"Proof I have to leave this town," I say.

"You always find proof of what you're looking for anyway. You made her God. But she's not God. She's just the woman who rejected you. I even remember your wife. She complained about you to strangers. She was gorgeous too wasn't she?" Dorothy Charles asks.

"What did she complain about?" I ask.

"She complained you weren't home enough. You had quite the drama going and now you're in jeans," she says.

"My ex-wife is in El Paso," I say.

"But you're not moving to El Paso," Dorothy Charles says.

"No," I say.

I wasn't the only one who went back to work that day. Big Larry went back to his construction company that afternoon. There was a welcome back party for him that didn't go well. No one realized the extent of his disability and his boss fired him permanently and sent him home.

"I w-w-worked with this guy coming up through the ranks for twelve y-years," Big Larry told Marvin.

"History of the World Part Two," Marvin said.

22

Unmarked Trailheads

I SAY TO WARREN, "A THERAPIST FRIEND TOLD ME GOD IS THE gorgeous woman who rejected me."

"No doubt," Warren says. "I've got lots of those Gods."

He sits back and sips his beer. "You're living with Gods right now, two of them, look at her," he says.

Natasha is on stage at a strip club in Lake Forest Park. "See this guy?" Warren whispers. "The closest he'll get to her is phone sex. But it's not stopping him from stuffing her with fives. I wish I was a chick."

Natasha's routine is winding down and everyone has her business card which she tosses in burlesque manner from the stage.

"You all so nice I thank you," she yells from the stage and soon we're getting into Warren's pickup.

"I make new customers tonight," she says, pulling herself up into the passenger seat. "Thank you for escorting me. I don't like do this. But business is slow so I do one time. Now new guys call for hot phone sex."

Warren says, "There's that guy. He followed us out."

"I make guys move," Natasha says. "They sit. They stand. They walk. They leave places and go places. Sometimes they run."

"I wish I was a chick," Warren says again and peels out of the neon lit parking lot past a cop car whose LED strobe lights immediately start flashing.

Moments later Warren is in front of the truck with his long arms stretched across the hood. Natasha jumps out and says, "Hey, Mister Police, it's me. This man not drunk, he's my twin sister's husband here protecting me. We local people like you."

The cop looks at her then looks again, inadvertently checking her out as she approaches. "Please, Ma'am, you'll have to wait in the vehicle," he says.

"But here is my card," she says, handing it to him, and he looks at it and says, "Intellectual phone sex?"

"I smart," she says. "My sister is anthropologist doctor realtor at university and not smart as me. My friend in car is psychiatrist."

"Actually I'm her husband," I say as the guy from the strip club walks closer and Natasha shakes her head and gives him the call me sign with her thumb and pinkie.

"You give phone sex too?" the cop asks him.

"No, Sir," he says.

"Then be on your way," the cop says then asks, "Whose animal is that?"

"Mine," Warren says.

"It's illegal to own a wolf in King County," he says.

"She's not a wolf," Warren says. "She's a Tervuren, a long-haired Belgian shepherd. Just looks like a wolf. They're police dogs in Amsterdam."

"And did she drink all these crushed beer cans back here?" the cop asks.

"Just retrieves them," Warren says.

"And always the same brand?" the cop says.

"She's discriminating," Warren says.

"There's a dumpster over there. Clean out the back of this pickup," the cop says and Natasha says, "Yes, Sir."

"Let him clean it out," the cop says.

He turns to Warren.

"The only reason you're getting off is because you're with her. Pull out slowly next time."

"Words to live by," Warren says and Natasha jumps up and down saying, "Oh, Mister Policeman, you so nice. Please call. I give you really smart intellectual phone sex. Here more cards for your station, for your police friends. Girls too I give great girl-to-girl intellectual phone sex. I will be so happy to hear from you."

Back in the truck Warren mimics, "Oh, Mister Policeman, you so nice," and Natasha says to me, "You so sweet to call me your wife. At last I am doctor's wife and not mentor doctor from Tacoma."

"You're a cop-magnet," I tell Warren.

We're driving around Kenmore and the north coast of Lake Washington. It's dark and thick with trees. Natasha says, "I was arrested in Tijuana because guys I was with had blow in motel room. They put me in cell and it was raining inside on me except it wasn't rain because when I looked up to see hole in roof Mexicans in next cell had climbed bars and were masturbating on me. I talked out of that one too, Warren."

"Well few people are smart but everyone has an education," Warren says. "Your sister needs me now for career advancement. I know the unmarked trailheads. She can't find them without me."

"She can find other Indian," Natasha says.

"Except now the faculty trusts me as its spirit guide," Warren says. "Your sister will save face by compromising with me. You'll see."

"The compromises we make are the sadness we bear," Natasha

says and Warren says, "She'll have sadness. Maybe it'll slow her down?"

I 405 South becomes I 90 East then Exit 27 arrives and we pass the casino. The woods grow deep. We wind around gravel roads and enter our gate. Julia is standing in the living room hands on hips.

"Why you here, Warren?" she demands.

"Because it's September and I come for you," he says. "I was here earlier but you were at the university so we escorted your sister to her gig and now we're back."

"Back where shouldn't be in first place," Julia says.

"Did you know your sister was masturbated on in Mexico?" he asks.

"What that got do with tea in China?" Julia asks.

"I figure I'd sleep here then take you on a hike tomorrow," he says. "There's a place almost nobody knows about except me. We can scope it out for the next faculty spiritual retreat."

"Oh you come on heavy now, Mister," Julia says and Warren smiles and says, "Maybe we can compromise on how we are together."

"There's beginning of end for you my friend," Julia says.

At four in the morning the ground is barely visible, the air is cool and the world is heavy. Warren drives us six miles from the house through North Bend and in from the truck stop up the middle fork of the Snoqualmie. Gravel flies behind us. When he stops it's as if we've gone deaf.

Warren says, "There's the official trailhead that way. That's where we send tourists."

"He's a good spirit guide," I whisper to Julia.

"We go this way instead," he says and slips down a steep embankment to the river. Then it's my turn. I catch my foot on a root and summersault twice to the river. I stand and conduct a mental body check.

Warren says, "September is a good month for rock finding.

Rocks will call to you. Look around. You can walk here from your house. It's a long walk but my point is this is your backyard. You're right on top of this and it's a different world. Look around. Welcome to nature."

We hike along the river until Warren points at something that isn't there and he dives into the underbrush. We follow and are instantly lost in deep forest.

"Listen for rocks," he whispers but there aren't any until we step in and out of a stream. We climb. Sometimes in the stream, sometimes beside the stream, and sometimes the stream disappears. I realize it's some sort of path. But it's so deep with ferns and moss and over-hanging growth that see-ground has almost disappeared again. Eventually Warren stops and sits.

"Here we are invisible," he says. "Only here."

"I think I know why I moved to Seattle," I say but no one asks me why. There is silence in this invisible place. A thing comes to me. When silence is more important than sharing, then you don't understand silence, because silence is sharing. This is what I hear. It's as if someone is talking to me. I won't be the one to break the silence. But it breaks when Natasha asks, "Why you move here?" and I say, "For my spiritual journey. I've been over-thinking myself. It's time to get a job."

"We celebrate you," Natasha says.

"It's true. We do," Warren says. "Spiritual journeys sneak up on people. It can take a long time before a journey gets to you. My advice is best to have a few good meals in the meantime so it won't be a total loss."

"Warren always makes funny man," Julia says and Warren says, "And I brought you here to this hidden womb of silence where ceremony is held without the aid of plant medicine, so we don't praise the door in favor of the room. I brought you here to the room itself. So that's the kind of funny man I am."

"What kind of job? Is it at hospital?" Natasha asks.

"We can have ceremony here with faculty!" Julia suddenly

shouts.

Natasha lets out a guffaw that hangs in the air like moisture.

Other sounds slip into the guffaw. Soon Warren's voice slips in saying "If you come in from a different direction, you can't find this place. You can only find it from the unmarked trailhead."

"Place of silence everywhere," Julia says.

"Just here," Warren says.

"Where is here?" Julia asks.

"Here is here," Warren says.

"Warren is right," I say. "When I was a kid we climbed Whiteface Mountain above Lake Placid. It was a long climb to the top and when we got there there were fat tourists who drove up the other side."

"Rip-off! Cheap shot!" Natasha shouts.

"It's not the same place when you come in from a different direction," Warren says.

"That was the year my dad died," I say. "It was his last summer. I saw him limp onto the dock kicking his artificial leg so the knee would lock, his sweet dignified smile almost like a glass of milk."

More silence.

"They gave us Donald Duck orange juice on the climb," I say.

More silence.

"The camp counselors," I say.

Julia asks, "How we charge if we not give medicine?"

Warren says, "Now you're thinking like a pusher. When did you become a pusher?"

More silence.

The fragmented feeling that is knowing circles us. Truth pours in. A slow video dissolve means time passing meaninglessly. It's like waiting. There is no undoing. There is done and move on. Then light shafts dive through the high branches. It's morning. Moisture lifts from the ground. I look at Natasha and she says to Julia, "Cloud lifts," right when I think it.

Warren says, "I don't do much. I get people to sit on the

ground."

Natasha says, "I think there is another silent spot ten feet away."

Warren says, "Only this one and only one way in."

"Through unmarked trailhead," Natasha says and Julia says, "I tell faculty," and she stands into the light.

"Silence is noisy," she says. "We find rocks now."

23

B-Roll

I'M IN A JOB INTERVIEW WALKING AROUND A PRIVATE MEDICAL facility to see if I'm the one the administrator Krista Charles will choose to do her video. Of course she's Dorothy Charles' sister.

"The president of the other company that is bidding sits on our Board," she's saying.

"How important is this video to you?" I ask.

"Important," she says.

"How important is he to you?" I ask.

She doesn't answer.

Farther down the corridor she says, "I can take care of him. He's devoted to the cause."

"Have you seen any of his previous work?" I ask.

"I haven't. He emailed me a file. We can access it from the conference room," she says.

"Your sister has some of my work. We can review his together right now if you want. What is he charging?" I ask.

"Twenty-two thousand dollars," she says and then she opens the conference room door, sits at the computer and activates the big screen.

"So?" she asks.

"So it just makes me wonder," I say.

"Now you need to be more specific," she says.

"I charge more," I say and Krista Charles says, "Pull up a chair. The video is only ten minutes long."

"That was a long ten minutes," I say when it's done. "Here's the short answer. I'll do the job for the same amount he quoted you. But I'll only do it if you watch the video again now and if you see what I see."

"Why would you lower your price?" Krista Charles asks.

"Three reasons," I say. "Your sister did me a favor in San Diego, a big favor for a friend of mine, a patient. I have a friend here that I want to train as my assistant and this will be a good job for her. And I don't want to charge you more than the guy you're not choosing *if* you're not choosing him. I don't want to come across like I'm moving him out to benefit me."

"Okay what should I look for?" she asks.

"Let me explain the standard technique first," I say. "I write a script with you and anyone else you designate. But we write the script in the hope of throwing it away piece by piece as the people we interview on screen accidentally say what was in the script they never got to see. My crew videos question and answer sessions with your key stakeholders. Then we delete the questions and string the answers together in donuts with B-roll. We only use voice-over talent when what was said in the live frame does not cover everything we had in the script."

"I have no idea what you just said," Krista Charles says. "What's B-roll?"

"I need you to understand what you are looking at. Then we can look at the video again," I say.

"I get that. So what's B-roll?" she asks again and I say, "B-roll is video without sound. It shows what a person is talking about. So if the voice is talking about shooting an arrow, B-roll shows someone shooting an arrow. Do you get that?"

"I do," she says.

"To understand B-roll you also have to understand a donut," I say.

"What's a donut?' she asks.

"A donut starts with someone's face talking," I say.

"Okay I get that," she says.

"Then keep the voice running but replace the face with B-roll about what that person is talking about. Then return to the person's face completing the thought. That's a donut," I say.

"I get it!" she says. "Person, B-roll, person equals donut."

"Correct and we string donuts together to make the video," I say.

"I understand now," Krista Charles says. "Thank-you for explaining."

"Now look at his video," I say. "There, see that, pause it. He stayed on the face too long. He didn't shoot enough B-roll so it wasn't in the can when he went to editing. It doesn't match up. The thought is lost. Do you see that? And there, look at the lighting. It's like the girl is wearing a lampshade."

"I see that," she says.

"So I'm not a fan of the production quality. It's distracting," I say. "And there is too much professional voice-over that removes the viewer from people who could be speaking from the living reality. There's too little B-roll to validate any story being told. The story itself, by the way, is coming across in a rather disjointed manner. The end result is the viewer is not drawn in. The viewer is just watching a poorly executed waste of time. What's that thing Louis Armstrong said? One cat can blow a thousand notes in a minute and say nothing and another cat can blow one note all night long and say it all. I think we're looking at nothing being said. Whoever paid for this paid too much. One more thing. This is the example he's proud of."

Krista Charles turns from the big screen and says, "Who are our key stakeholders?"

I say, "Former and present patients, their families, doctors, nurses, administration, your board and major donors. We can move the viewer from the hospital infrastructure to the patient, to the families, to the community."

She points the remote at the big screen and turns it off.

"I see what you see," she says. "When can you start?"

24

Bat Time

"HIS WORK WASN'T GOOD," I TELL NATASHA. "BUT I DIDN'T want it to look like I was crapping on the guy just so we could get the job," and she says. "What you mean *we* can get job?"

"I want you to be my production assistant," I say.

"We win award and trophy?" she asks, closing her laptop. "I get on stage and say thank-you mother?"

"A charred bridge," I say. "Sometimes I see my life as a rush back across charred bridges."

'"You smart salesman. You not like money?" she says. "I need money."

"That's why I'm doing this," I say

"It is?" she asks. "For me? How we do video? You teach me. What my job is? Oh you are best man."

"You're the coordinator," I say. "You'll make sure everyone I need shows up on time wearing what I want them to wear."

"Who is everyone?" she asks.

"I don't know yet? I say.

"When you know?" she asks.

"I'll know after I write the script with Doctor Krista Charles," I say.

"When you do that?" she asks.

"Next week," I say.

"What I do until then?" she asks.

"I'll send you back and forth to get information once I have my list together," I say.

"What list?" she asks.

"The list of people to video and what they'll talk about and why," I say.

"When you have list?" she asks.

"This is exhausting," I say.

"But I need to know. You give me marketable skill and new career. I am serious," she says. "Email me list of whole process so I study to learn and not be exhausting."

"That's a good suggestion. I'll do that tonight," I say.

"Warren at house tonight to see Julia maybe he want video for faculty spirit quest business? Video of silent place, a no-talkie," she laughs.

"I'm sorry I called you exhausting. I didn't mean you. I meant explaining myself," I say.

"You never say sorry. What wrong with you?" she asks. "No Indian word for sorry."

"Who told you that, Warren? Did he think it to you in the silent place?" I ask.

"That would be good movie!" she says. "He told me in truck when he thought I was my sister."

"I thought you weren't your sister," I say.

"So what is intention for video?" she asks.

"Krista Charles needs to raise awareness and funds," I say. "It's always like that in these places. It's a private medical facility. This one does therapy for catastrophic brain injury patients. The government just got out of these long term care facilities so there's no government money or at least there is less government money. Krista Charles needs private donors to sustain the medical facility as a nonprofit. You know what the patients do?"

"What they do?" she asks.

"They fill things like spice jars," I say. "The medical facility has a sales force. It gets contracts from companies. The patients work and get paid a salary as their therapy for long term care. That's where we come in. People need to see the video and give money to sustain the hospital. So the intention is an appeal. Close-ups, sincerity, immediacy, pull at the heart strings, tears in the eyes, reach for the wallet."

"So what I do?" she asks again.

"I need a list of everyone who will be on camera," I say. "That includes administration, government officials, major donors, staff, doctors, patients and patient family members. You can get the list from Doctor Krista Charles. Call her tomorrow."

"But how I talk to her?" she asks.

"I'll write down exactly the way I want you to ask her," I say. "I'll follow up with an email and copy you. We will shoot for three days. I'll need you to get dates from Doctor Charles and a schedule of who will appear when, solid colors for clothes, change of outfits no stripes. From those people, I'll string together a story of need and concern. I'll write a questionnaire for each person, but meanwhile I'll hire a cinematographer with broadcast digital equipment and a lighting and sound crew and an editor who uses Final Cut Pro software. We'll edit for two days. I'll also want you to scope locations. I'll go with you to show you what works and what doesn't."

"This is serious," she says. "I am so happy."

"Hey, Swims with Parakeets," Warren says, walking in the front door. "It's getting dark out. Have you noticed that it was summer today? That's what we say in the Pacific Northwest. Summer is a handful of nonconsecutive days strung together. Well, in case you didn't notice, today was summer."

"It was fall," Julia says, walking in behind him. "It is September. I was in classroom. Then I had meeting with chair."

"Not with a table?" Warren asks.

"He interested in special place of silence," Julia says, removing her jacket.

"I have more news for you," Warren says. "Phil McPherson just flew back from Peru with San Pedro cactus. We can conduct a long dance."

"These Port Angeles people cowboys. What is San Pedro cactus? What is long dance? We sit on floor you tell us," Julia says and sits cross-legged on the carpet.

"September everything is business," Natasha says. "September, September, September, I am new video coordinator for medical facility video shoot and streaming media."

"I realtor Assistant Professor Anthropology," Julia says.

They hug each other and Warren removes his shoes and sits cross-legged, completing the circle.

Warren says, "Insane, soul-crushing women turn you inside out. Hey-hi-yah-ah-nah-chi-oh. Bat time." He points at the window. "Sun is down, bats are out. See how quiet is the light for feeding. You know what bat time is? If you think you saw it, it was a bat. That's bat time."

"I think it past your bat time, Warren," Julia says.

"No, look, almost didn't see it again," he says and points to the window and we look.

Natasha says, "It's true. I almost see it."

"Bat time," Warren says.

"Long dance?" Julia asks.

Afterimages of bats swoop and dive for mosquitoes in front of Mount Si. Warren says, "San Pedro cactus comes from the Andes. You brew a few quills in a cup and you go to places you never considered. You make it easy or hard on yourself by dancing and drumming around a fire the whole night. Phil McPherson came back with a shaman from there. They chose a place near Grays Harbor. First we conduct place of silence this weekend as a pre-training ground for the faculty. Then next weekend we will conduct the long dance."

"How much we charge?" Julia asks.

"Three hundred per person," Warren says.

"Look, didn't see again!" Natasha shouts.

"Bat time," Warren says. "You should see them on the fourth of July. They get disoriented and fly at picture windows."

"Do they get disoriented or do the mosquitoes?" Natasha asks.

25

Joe's Hand

PALM TREES IN CREST AREN'T LIKE THE PALM TREES IN BEVERLY
Hills. They don't have swan necks. They have dead grass skirts
where rats live. The sun strikes the palm trees and they shower dust.
The dust hangs in the air. Sun filters through the dust like in a
religious painting and that happy-for-no-reason thing appears.
But its dust and it floats to the ground and becomes the dirt of the
high desert.

Today the tree trimmers are working up the street so the dust
is heavy as Roxanne walks down the middle of the street through
the light shafts. Joe steps out of his geodesic dome and sees her.
Marvin stops work on the Avanti in Big Larry's driveway and Big
Larry balances on two canes by the compost pile. Roxanne stops
to talk to him. Buster the puppy scratches at a late September flea.

"Incoming!" Marvin shouts and Dorothy Charles pulls her
black Suburban into the driveway.

Big Larry starts limping up the road with Roxanne and Joe.

When they get to the driveway, Roxanne gently guides Big Larry by placing her hand on his back.

"Ca-cat fight," Big Larry says. "I hope."

"Who are you?" Roxanne asks Dorothy Charles and Dorothy Charles says, "Oh, you must be Roxanne. I've heard so much about you. I'm Dorothy Charles. I worked with your boyfriend at the hospital."

"Oh, he's not my boyfriend," Roxanne says. "We don't put names to things up here."

"Except that's oleander," Big Larry says, pointing one of his canes.

"Comes in lots of colors, reds, yellows, oranges," Joe says. "All poisonous. I mean horses take a chomp boom down."

Dorothy Charles turns to me.

"I wanted to see what's going on up here," she says.

"Just chips and salsa and how about beer, you want some beer, Pacifico with lime?" Marvin asks from Big Larry's fence. "Get some from his place. Go around the back of the main house. I'll be there as soon as I wash up."

"That'll be a first," Big Larry says.

Then the group makes its way slowly around the rockery to the back porch with the overhanging blue Jacaranda growing up the middle of it.

"There's the cabin," I tell Dorothy Charles, pointing across the property, and she asks, "That's where you do your work?"

"For all the good it does," Joe says.

"B-b-bust my sander," Big Larry tells her.

"Pacifico slices of lime," Marvin calls out from the kitchen.

"So bring them," Joe shouts then says to Dorothy Charles, "So what did you do at that hospital?"

"I'm still there. I'm a doctor," she says.

"Look at my hand," Joe says. "Can you prescribe or are you just a pretend sort of therapist doctor?"

"What kinds of stories have you been telling up here about

therapists?" Dorothy Charles asks me.

Buster suddenly bounds onto the porch and Roxanne calls into the house, "Marvin, puppy came to find you!"

"M-must have l-left the gate open," Big Larry says.

"Goats will get out," Joe says.

"I'll check it," Marvin says, putting the beers on the dowel.

Buster runs after him.

Dorothy Charles says, "This is a healthy place, a healthy community," and Big Larry says, "H-h-health is like a smile. You c-can't keep it on your face all the time. It hurts."

"What about my hand?" Joe asks.

Dorothy Charles is still holding it.

"I'm glad I'm here," she says.

"We're glad you're here too," Roxanne says.

"Wait until you see how beautiful that cabin is," I say and Big Larry says, "Ha-ha-hundred year old f-floors."

"I knew I closed that door," Marvin says, coming back. "He's getting out some other way. Buster is really smart."

"Of course he is," Roxanne says.

"Show me the cabin," Dorothy Charles says.

"What about my hand?' Joe asks.

"You have to pay to go in there," Marvin says.

"Unless you're a hooker, are you a hooker?' Joe asks.

"I'm a doctor," Dorothy Charles says.

"Then my hand?" Joe asks.

"All right let me see. This hand doesn't look good," she says.

"What's wrong with it?"Joe asks.

"I don't know. It just doesn't look good," she says.

"She means it's ugly," Marvin says.

"I'm a therapist," Dorothy Charles says.

"Not another one," Joe sighs.

Buster runs toward the east eucalyptuses and Marvin calls him back, turns to Dorothy Charles and says, "Rattlesnakes use gofer holes like highways. That's my boy, Buster. I'm borrowing a tractor to dig down and level that whole area."

"Well, plans are productive because they place you in forward thinking mode. Work is healing," Dorothy Charles says.

"Christ almighty," Marvin sighs. "Can't you talk like an ordinary person with simple language? We should build a fire and roast your thoughts."

"I won't be here that late," she tells him and walks into the cabin. She closes the door and it's just her and me inside.

I say, "Up here people just show up. Friends, enemies, it doesn't matter. People don't call. It's considered rude to call. Everyone in Crest is in walking distance. Everyone walks over if they have something to say. But you on the other hands are not from up here so you should have called."

She doesn't answer.

She walks around touching things like the computer, the desk, the chairs and the table. At last she says, "Nice floor."

"And how did you find me anyway?" I ask.

"Do you think it's hard to find anyone anymore?" she asks. "I drove up and went to that store you call a town. I gave your name and got here."

"And you're here because..." I ask.

"How can you leave this place? It's glorious. This room is glorious. Your friends are cool. Roxanne is spectacular. I could be your friend here," she says.

"And you're here because..." I repeat and she says, "I can deflect patients your way, patients that I believe need more of a natural grounding than a hospital or a couch. If you're interested in having a practice, or expanding this practice, I wanted to see your setup."

"It looks like this," I say and Dorothy Charles suddenly starts to laugh. "You think Joe just wanted me to hold his hand?"

"I wouldn't let his wife know that," I say. "I believe it hurts him. He's completely straight forward."

"I don't know. Maybe there's some arthritis," Dorothy Charles says, "But Roxanne certainly got territorial."

"Yeah, wasn't that great!" I say.

"You have protectors again," she says.

"I do," I say.

"And they have you," she says. "And by the way," she says, opening the door, "You're not leaving for Seattle so fast even though you know approximately where she is now," and she walks out because there's some commotion at the giant jades. Two police cars are stopped in front of Big Larry's house and Marvin is being shuffled into one of them.

"There's someone we need him to identify," one of the officers says.

"At the *morgue!*" an old woman shouts from inside one of the police cars. "I ain't going there *alone!*"

"That's his aunt," Joe says to me.

"A bit of arthritis," I tell him.

"Where he's going I'm going," Roxanne tells the cops.

"We'll take my Suburban," Dorothy Charles says, and, at the morgue, Marvin is looking at his brother on a slab. The old aunt, dusty and decrepit, is sobbing into her flannel shirt. A detective, a couple of uniformed officers and a technician have positioned themselves next to the slab. Roxanne, I and Dorothy Charles are against the wall. Marvin just stares at his brother.

"Can you identify him?" the detective asks again and Marvin just stares.

"See the slice on his palm," the detective says. "He felt the knife slicing across his throat from behind so he reached for the knife and it sliced his hand and his throat at the same time."

Marvin doesn't say anything.

The detective says, "You know who did it, don't you?"

Roxanne places her arm on Marvin's shoulder.

"What the fuck?" Marvin shouts.

"We'll pray," Roxanne says.

"Drug deal gone wrong," the detective says. "There's a lot of bad stuff that goes down here in San Diego."

"Heavenly Father," Roxanne begins.

"Look at his palm," Marvin says, holding it up to Roxanne. "I can see it going down. I can see it right now."

26

Long Dance

THE CAMERA IS ROLLING AND KRISTA CHARLES SAYS, "BETTER
be careful while driving or someday you may be working for
me."

And there it is. In her mind, these patients stuffing spice jars
are working for her, paying her salary. That's how Krista Charles
sees it. That's it, right there, the hidden reality the camera always
uncovers. As soon as she says it, I know I'll see it again in post and
have to decide to edit it out or keep it in. She says it and everything
stops for me even though her mouth keeps moving.

I'm standing next to the camera, so she's speaking into my
eyes. I ask the questions, she answers, and the camera captures her
saying, "Better be careful driving or someday you may be working
for me."

"I wonder if I'll have the courage to leave it in," I say to Natasha
at the Starbucks around the corner.

"In where?" she asks.

"In the final edit," I say.

"Why would you not?" she asks.

"Competing allegiances," I say. "I promised to make her look good. I'm supposed to protect her."

"Protect from what?" she asks.

"From what she says that she doesn't realize," I say.

"You like Doctor Krista Charles?" she asks.

"Not really," I say.

"Not now," she asks.

"Correct," I say.

"So what you do?" she asks.

"First I have to complete the process," I say.

"What you do in process?" she asks.

"We filmed all the interviews first," I say.

"For the donut," she says.

"Correct and tomorrow we'll film B-roll," I say. "But I also asked everyone for a stinger."

"What is stinger? I like that name."

"It's a moment I use after the video is over. Sometimes it's a summary statement. Sometimes I ask for a stinger that just says *thank you* that I can piece together in post. So it's different people, thank-you, thank-you, thank-you, thank-you or summary statement, summary statement, summary statement, summary statement at the end of the video. It's just a bunch of linked thoughts at the end. Or maybe it's just one thought. You've seen them. Sometimes an outtake is used, usually in cheap productions. So I just capture them in the shoot in case I use them later and that's how the camera caught Krista Charles. That's how she caught herself. Sometimes I don't even use a stinger. So why should I automatically use it? I just always want to have something extra in the can in case I decide to use it. If it's not in the can you can't edit in later what's not there to begin with."

"Professional language very sexy," Natasha says. "I thank you for explaining because you are good explainer, but now you must use it. Like you told me, you ask what they think they are then film *what* they are. How Warren say in ceremony? Sit by the river and wait. Your enemy's corpse will soon float by."

"I could place the clip on the home page of the website," I say. "Better be careful driving or someday you may be working for me. Shoving it forward like that becomes branding. But it would be so wrong for me to brand her that way. Powerful though, that would be powerful branding. Nobody ever went broke underestimating the taste of the general public."

At the table next to us an insurance executive with a Bluetooth in his ear is talking to a trainee and saying, "Here's the way we do it. Repeat after me, people in your situation usually choose..." and the trainee says, "People in your situation usually choose..."

The insurance executive says, "That's good," and Natasha leans into me and whispers, "I vomit now."

"Now you're the camera," I say.

"How is that?" she asks.

"So am I. I must tell you. I'm smarter than I let on," I say.

"That's how camera is? Camera is *I'm smarter than I let on*?" she asks and I say, "Yes."

"Why?" she asks.

"People only show themselves when you let them slip you into the background. That's when they give it up," I say.

"Give what up?" she asks.

"That thing inside truth," I say.

"What thing?" she asks.

"The part they don't even know about themselves," I say. "And the dumb camera captures it all because it's smarter than it lets on."

"People in your situation usually choose," she says and I say, "To sit by the river," and she says, "And Doctor Krista Charles float by."

"B-roll tomorrow," I say.

"Place of Silence Saturday," Natasha says. "Forecast rain."

"This ceremony of silence is your door to the Long Dance,"

Warren says to the group as it enters the unmarked trailhead.

It's a cold morning still dark. The participants are not yet fully awake and have their hoods up. I can see their breath. They move low and dark through the underbrush. Soon Warren motions to a hole in a long row of blackberry bushes.

Everyone moves through head down. There are twelve people from the university, Julia's coworkers, bosses and honored guests. Warren indicates nothing and nobody makes a sound. A cough is heard. All five types of followers are present. The sheep are here. The yes people are here. The alienated are here. The pragmatist survivors are here. The better-safe-than-sorry are here. The star followers are here. Soon there's a sense of moaning. Warren think-says, "Regret brings a person to no good end. Letting go of regret frees your spirit. Letting go of regret is healthy living."

"Ah-ho," Julia think-says.

Rain is on the branches. A bird chirps.

We make our way along the stream that appears and disappears. We find and lose the trail that is barely a trail. Tundra the gray ghost dog is out there somewhere protecting the periphery. Eventually Warren points us into a small enclosure. Everyone sits in a tight, wet, dark circle. I'm sitting on a round piece of wood the size of my palm. I fall into Natasha to pull it from under me and put it in my pocket. My shuffling creates a domino effect like a tear in the circle. People rearrange themselves. Another cough is heard.

"Bear jerky," Warren think-says.

"Ah-ho," Julia think-says.

"Bear jerky," Warren repeats. I see him look around the circle. See-ground has manifested. He says, "Bear eat garbage. Hunter shoots bear. Meat stinks. Add lots of spices. Make into sticks. Camouflage taste and smell. Bear jerky. Bear jerky government. Bear jerky television. Bear jerky wars. Bear jerky jobs."

"Ah-ho," Julia think-says.

More silence.

"They'll come for *me* now," Marvin the Mobile Mechanic says.

"Maybe they'll get you too by mistake. Aren't you scared?"

"Not since Swims with Horses," I say.

"What's that supposed to mean?" he asks.

"It means nothing has mattered for a while, not since everything mattered," I say and he says, "You mean something has to matter before you're scared?"

"That's why you're scared," I tell him.

"Well your car is done, so I guess we're even," he says.

More silence.

"That what Arlo Guthrie told me in Maui," Natasha says. "He told me when you know you know. But lots of people don't know. Some know. But everyone knows when you know-when-you-know. But you can't fake know when you know, not to those who know when they know."

More silence.

"Sure," Dorothy Charles says. "Nobody wants to hurt anybody. But hurt has its own rules."

"Then not play game if not no rules," Natasha says and Swims with Horses says, "I guess that's true. Though you can't control the direction of the wind, you can always adjust your sails."

"Ah-ho," Julia think-says.

More silence.

I say to Warren, "I don't care who sings Somewhere Over the Rainbow, that person is off my list," and Warren asks, "Off what list?"

"The list of valid anything, anybody," I say.

"What if it's Swims with Horses?" he asks.

"Off my list," I say.

"We'll have to get her to sing that for you," he says.

"Ah-ho," Julia think-says.

Then sometime in the future Natasha steps over me, then Julia steps over me, and I reach up and touch her leg as she passes. Then one of the faculty gets to his knees and moves out low, and I realize the place of silence is being vacated. It's like water pouring out of a glass.

Only Warren and I are left.

You come out of winter like from a dark room on a moving train. You move unsteadily down the narrow corridor knowing that something is still on you, something you're still on. Maybe later you stand drained on a cold platform and the train pulls away from you. We stand and stretch in the forest.

Everyone is just standing around.

Eventually Warren says, "Because you experienced the place of silence you can attend the Long Dance next week."

"Welcome to the Long Dance!" Warren shouts at Grays Harbor and he points to his banner on a chain-link fence. Everyone else's banner is on that fence too. His is a green towel with 25% painted in white in the middle of it, surrounded by many hawk feathers stuck in the towel.

A flock of herons swoops in over the swamp and our snapping fire. The herons descend in circular formation with their legs trailing. They look like aircraft carriers. Around and around they glide, lower and lower, then out of site into bat time. Mosquitoes rise. The snapping fire sends chunks of debris at the banners on the chain-link fence and Warren turns back from the herons and shouts, "Before the dance all of you were asked to paint something to depict your intention for the dance. Maybe what you want to leave behind. Maybe what you want to call in. It's a banner of who you are so we can know each other. Twenty-five percent," he says, now pointing at his banner.

He pauses.

"That's how much Indian blood you must have to be a tribal member. I've been thinking about this. I've been working on the equation. Some may say the wisdom, the intention, is what I've been working on. I've been gathering an understanding in anticipation of being here in front of you. Some white guy rapes your great grandmother. That's okay, that happens when you're being annihilated, not her fault. Now that offspring, your grandfather, is fifty percent. Now he chooses a white woman. Well, love is love, let's say we'll give you one of those, and they have a nice little girl, your mother, and that's twenty-five percent. Now your mother marries a white guy and you know that's a little too far down that road with those who wiped us off the face of the earth. You know, that's too far down the white road. We'll give you one for being violated in war, one for love, but that's it. After that, it's below twenty-five percent and you don't get to be a tribal member. Hey sure we got beaten but you have to hold on to something, and that's me just below twenty-five percent. You see me, I'm all Indian, but not to the tribe. I don't get those casino benefits and I'm not like you either. That's my banner. I was born not to get into the one place I belong. I'm the final solution. Who wants to talk next?"

Frank Sid, hairy black arms and bald head, goes to the chain-link fence. He holds up a piece of plywood and says, "This is my banner. I was crabbing at Dutch Harbor out around Priest Rock. It's a rock that looks like a priest and when you come around it you're in the full force of the Bering Sea. We were in thirty foot swells and the window broke and the water was gushing in. I went below to my bunk and had this piece of plywood under it. It fit almost exactly into the window. It was as close as I've come to death. It's amazing how quickly you can fill up with water when the whole ocean is pouring in."

"Asshole," I say, holding up my banner. It's a white sheet with Asshole painted on it. "I watched her get it wrong about me that I was an asshole and everything I did to show her differently proved her right. That was the equation she had me in."

"People think I am asshole too," Natasha says, holding up her banner, "but I am Medical Cinematographer Production Assistant Pole Dancer Telephone Sexologist. I am smarter than I let on and my camera sees more because it not judges. That why I paint medical symbol on pink camera thank-you."

Banner after banner and soon Warren says, "We dance all

night in the circle around this fire. Half the night we dance in one direction then we switch directions to dance toward morning."

Meanwhile Phil McPherson is squatting over the fire, watching the tea brew, the tea with needles of San Pedro cactus in it.

"It's called achuma," he says to the first person in line. "It's the sacred cactus of the Andes."

It's a long line of perhaps forty people. Phil McPherson hands up one cup at a time. Some people struggle to keep the liquid down. The shaman begins to play two flutes in his mouth at the same time.

We're dancing and have been for three hours. The circle is muddy from all the stomping. The night is black. The swamp air is thick. Frank Sid passes me, pounding his drum and limping with fatigue. He's struggling in the dance. His legs are heavy. Phil McPherson passes me, dancing and drumming on his beautifully hand-painted elk drum with its white cedar rim. Almost everyone has a beautiful elk drum. All I have is a stick for a striker and the block of wood the size of my palm that I was sitting on in the place of silence.

Now Natasha stomps past me doing her Tuli Kuperferberg imitation, "Monday nothing, Tuesday nothing, Wednesday nothing, Thursday nothing." She passes my Asshole banner on the chain-link and starts giggling. I follow her to get into her drumming style. My stick strikes my hand as often as it strikes the block of wood. I make a ti-tick, ti-tick, ti-tick sound as I march along.

Dragon Spirit Fire from Las Cruces gets between us with a different beat that's agonizingly labored but paradoxically gives me a second wind. The athlete in me takes over. I pound past her and Natasha. The love of movement has energized me. I have a new beat on my swollen hand, a faster beat, a happy beat. It frees me. Movement is everything. Everything is great as long as I'm moving. It's as if I'm wearing rollerblades. I dance like I'm skating.

"What was the gentlest touch you ever gave? Oh, that's easy, to Swims with Horses under her tennis shorts in my office. That's correct, Contestant Two, and you can now move on to Level Five and the question what would be the ultimate test of second chances? Ever returning to San Diego, that's correct, and now to Level Six and finish this statement, nobody ever wants to hurt anybody, but... Correct, hurt has its own rules."

"What is glue?" Dragon Spirit Fire from Las Cruces asks, holding up her banner. "Ideological glue, physiological glue, spiritual glue, that's what's on my banner, a glob of glue."

The night moves within itself through endless drumming, endless walking and endless dancing around and around the mud circle while the fire snaps debris at us like flaming cockroaches in the swamp night. And the night is also endless trudging to different beats and endless pantomime people to follow and pass. Drumming, I can do that. I can drum. It's in me now to drum. I must remember when this is over to get a drum. I'm running now and splashing up mud as I pass everyone, Sea Biscuit along the rail. My Rollerblades glide through the dry parts, the sawdust parts, like I'm skating the boardwalk mile after mile passing everyone, even those on bicycles, all the way to where Loring dead-ends at the ocean. And Swims with Horses asks, "Why destroy yourself?" and now I know why.

We're sitting by the tennis courts at Torrey Pines where I'll propose to her and she'll say yes even though we're both married to someone else, but we're pulled together, pulled like a runner's inward breath pulling him forward, *that* kind of running, *that* kind of pulling, pulling us together and I say, "Other women have been in love with me. They get all broken up. Why aren't you all broken up?" and she says, "Why destroy yourself?" and now I know why. It's to clear out all that's wrong and not to worry about what else might go in the process because what's right grows back first. I could have said that. I say that now as I run through the mud. When you're in love you clear yourself of all that's wrong and that's why you get all broken up in pieces. There are gaps in the sculpture of you and you move around crumbling. All broken up, all broken up, I say it as I run and Swims with Horses says, "You know the joke about the old bull and the young bull. They're on a knoll looking down on a herd of cattle. The young bull says let's run down and fuck a cow, and the old bull says why don't we walk down and fuck them all. I guess I'm an old bull."

Julia has a weird drumming style like the way she chops vegetables into small pieces.

Small pieces, she drums, small pieces.

She points at my banner and Warren's banner and says, "See you and Warren same spirits both final solutions. But see my banner. Here is new solution. Here this tree represent I marry logger to come to this country but treat me bad so I wait for citizenship papers then divorce him, get education and now free in this wonderful country so tree fall and new tree grows, tree of me in graduation cap anthropologist associate professor and in corner real estate cards, I get you homes and make you free too."

I'm drumming with her, chopping into tiny vegetables, and the needles of San Pedro make her appear like a long-legged, long-boned queen from some distant planet. But those choppy beats get tiresome. They let weariness in. She leaves the circle and I follow her toward the deep forest. I don't have the strength to pull away. She's not dancing. She's not drumming. She's walking into the woods. She's going to pee, to squat somewhere past a mound where Warren has placed his torso-sized crystal. I catch it in my peripheral vision and stop. There she is. There it is. There it all is. I dropped to my knees in front of the mound.

Swims with Horses is alive inside the crystal. She's talking to me. That precise voice, crisp intelligence, quiet humor, angelic face and brilliant, sexy, funny, athletic, positive, cold natural beauty.

"You rose an eagle," Warren says, "but that's not how we say it. An eagle rose for you. That's how we say it because the eagle decides. Actually we just say an eagle rose. I've never seen that except for cancer patients. So what makes you so desperately worthy?"

I say to Swims with Horses, "I never forgot. I'll always be in love with you."

"That's when the eagle rose," Warren says. "I saw it. It's the message carried from the soul to the soul. Mission accomplished, Asshole."

I turn around to him and he's not there. Instead Julia comes out of the bushes and I turn back to the crystal and Swims with Horses is gone, fading back, back, back and gone.

I return to the circle and dancers are now dancing in the other direction. It's midpoint in the long dance, the depth of night, and Dragon Spirit Fire from Las Cruces has found her beat. I drum behind her. Oh, she didn't like to hike into the Andes using horses, but it was the only way to go in that deep. They needed the extra supplies. Now her stride is confident and happy. The Mercy touch is what the Sisters of Mercy called it the way comfort is bestowed. I feel that touch in Dragon Spirit Fire's stride and in her drumming. I am the recipient of the Mercy touch and an eagle rose. We are all in the middle of the place we can't penetrate.

"Who's Asshole?" Dragon Spirit Fire from Las Cruces asks, shielding her eyes from the morning sun.

I begin to raise my hand hesitantly but then think that really it's not something to admit.

"He is," Warren says.

"I'm not. That's the point," I say.

"Is this your banner?" Warren asks.

"Summarizer," I say.

"I want to thank you. I mean I thank you," Dragon Spirit Fire from Las Cruces says. "Whatever thoughts I had in my head whenever I passed the asshole banner it made me laugh at myself. Asshole I said and then I gained clarity. So thank you for your stunning banner."

"You always attract the pretty ones," Natasha says as we walk away from the circle.

"Oh, this is like I'm married again," I say and Warren says, "You had a jealous wife."

"Oh, yes," I say.

"I am not jealous," Natasha says. "What is jealous?"

"You mean the crossroads where boredom meets insecurity?" Warren asks then adds, "Crosshairs is more like it."

Dragon Spirit Fire runs up to me and says, "It's you, isn't it? He has the shiny long black hair and the hawk feathers in his towel and arranges the ceremonies but it's you. It's you isn't it? You're the one. You're the healer. You dropped this," and she shoves the block of wood into my hand, my drum.

"Oh, thanks," I say, looking at the drum.

"Your hand is all cut up," she says.

"It is," I say, looking at it.

"You don't make decisions for people. That's why you're the one," she says and runs off.

"What do you make of that?" Warren asks.

"I think she's right," I say. "You're the one with the hawk feathers in your towel."

"You never even see me when we dance," Natasha says to me. "But I see you follow Julia into woods. I see you dance so fast."

"Because I go pee," Julia says, catching up to us.

"You go past us so fast. You dance like burning rocket," Natasha says to me.

We see the pickup.

Warren says, "The problem with ceremonies is you only attract complainers so you can't make real money because complainers are mostly poor. But this university crowd, they're complainers with money. I can separate them from the others. Thank you, Julia."

"You help make me look good, Warren," she says. "You give me secrets of other people. Faculty talks in whispers about experiences. I am important person on campus now."

"Our son will have eight point five percent Indian blood," Warren says. "He'll be a secret roadman healer like Asshole here."

"No son. No daughter. No eight point five percent. Your math wrong, Warren," Julia says. "Maybe tribe just don't want you."

"Hoy, what a woman. Sell any real estate in the long dance?"

he asks. "Look people are turning on their cell phones. They're scrolling up and down and across. Good time for you to send out a promotional email linked to a newsletter and a gift."

"Warren, that's good idea," she says.

"I was joking," he says, getting in the truck and dropping his head to the wheel.

I lean in the driver's side window and whisper, "Do you have cancer, Warren?" and he says, "It's a good crystal, isn't it? There's another kind I want to get when I have enough money, but this one is a good one."

27

Spice Scooping

"THEY'LL COME FOR ME NOW," MARVIN THE MOBILE MECHANIC
says. "Maybe they'll get you by mistake at the same time.
Aren't you scared?"

"Not since everything mattered," I say.

"What's that supposed to mean?" he asks.

"It means everything hasn't mattered for a long time," I say.

"You mean everything has to matter for you to be scared?" he
asks.

"That's why you're scared," I tell him.

"Well your car is done, so I guess we're even," he says and
he breaks into song as if in a musical, "Somewhere... over the
rainbow... bluebirds fly..." and everyone in front of the spice bin
turns to the camera and sings, "There's a land that I dreamed of
once in a lullaby..."

"What you thinking?" Natasha asks.

I pull my eye back from the camera and say, "My mind was

wandering. B-roll is boring. Maybe that's what the B stands for. I need to be more in the present."

"We all need that," Natasha says.

Just then Krista Charles walks into the auditorium and surveys the chaos that is video setup. She hesitates, letting her eyes do her walking. Now she walks in her high heels and the sound echoes off the floor and the walls. The crew turns to take her in. She steps across lighting wires and camera cables and past the open equipment cases. Before she gets to us she satisfies whatever questions she has so when she arrives all she asks is, "How was your weekend?"

"I debunked my ambivalence," I say and Natasha says, "We were on Olympic Peninsula at a dance."

"You dance?" Krista Charles asks me.

"I do," I say.

"Well I went to a luncheon on Saturday and raised money for new manufacturing equipment," she says. "I'll let you and your crew back to-"

"B-roll," Natasha says. "We shoot more B-roll today," and Krista Charles steps away as if from a flame, turns and leaves and Natasha says, "We never have our best conversations alone. It's always with others around when you mention things that are profound. We should change that."

"You thought that was a good conversation?" I ask and she says, "Debunk your ambivalence. I want to talk that with you, not hear you say to her."

"You shouldn't be so obvious in showing your dislike for her," I say. "You should be more invisible. That's how she likes you. She can see you're smart and beautiful."

"I am?" Natasha asks and a smile crawls on her face. "See you so nice. You are best man."

"So how was *your* weekend?" I ask and she says, "Oh, this is good me-you-only conversation. I tell you just because it called ceremony it still means drugs. Warren say drugs conduit to understanding everyone does it, keep elderly population alive. Warren say complainers are poor people but really he mean drug addicts are poor people, drug-addicts-complainer-poor-people. Warren has pusher mentality. He is good at finding the thing and then he pushes that thing. He pushes that thing into Julia. Watch her. Warren finds her thing. He addicts her to that thing. That thing esteem at university. He pushes that one on her. Indians don't even do these ceremonies. These invented for white man to pay for ceremonies. Indians don't pass talking stick. Indians don't do mushroom ceremony. Indians don't do long dance ceremony. These inventions for white people to pretend not doing drugs. That why they say plant medicine, great creator plant spirit plant medicine, anyway was my weekend, I look around. I see."

"Thanks to drugs," I say.

"That funny, no, really, that funny, but I see. I s-e-e," she says. "I don't need drugs to see truth about drugs."

"What about the Port Angeles group?" I ask. "Have you noticed how the Port Angeles group has fallen into the scenery?"

"I notice," she says.

"Do you s-e-e why?" I ask.

"They drug addicts," she says.

"A professional like Dr. Charles' younger sister might say it differently," I say. "She might say there's a dulling to the personality invoked by redundant activity. The personality sprouts unfocused edges and begins to fade when exposed to redundant activity."

"Drug addicts," Natasha says. "Like I say and Warren knows. That why Warren wants separate them from faculty. Oh, this is a good me-you-only conversation!" and I say, "But if you think this is a good conversation, wait until we get into the post-production room and the engineer starts searching for a scene. Wait until we see the thing we thought we saw."

"Bat time!" Natasha says and I say, "It's all going to be bat time in post production."

While we're talking the mentally and physically disabled B-roll stars are being moved into place in front of the large communal spice bin. Wheelchairs are bounced over cables and wiring. But once in their places the patients start scooping spice into jars. Some need help from a handler to accomplish the scooping. One is blind and must feel when the jar is full. A girl with straw hair in a ponytail uses a wood and metal jig to support her arm in the scooping task. They all wear thin plastic gloves that get pulled on one way then the other and soon don't fit right. The camera zooms in and out capturing the face, the hand, the process, the face, the hand, the process, the jar, the scoop, the face, the bin, the spice, zoom in on spice, pull back on spice, the jar, the hand, the jig, the face, the bin. Loose spice is scooped into glass jars. Tops are screwed on glass jars. Labels are affixed. Focus in close, but don't show labels. Pull back. Do it again.

"And how was your weekend?" Natasha asks me and I step back from the camera.

"I'm glad you care about your sister and you watch over her," I say.

"We have big fight coming," she says and I say, "I was energized as an athlete. It was wonderful like a good memory."

"Quiet on the set!" the lighting guy yells at us because he's a jokester and there's no sound in B-roll, maybe just some ambient sound.

He smiles over at me and yells it again.

I ask Natasha, "Do you think people in non-profits should be compensated less than people who just sell stuff in big corporations?"

"Yes they should make less," she says.

"The money should go to the cause?" I ask.

"Yes," she says.

"So fundraising is pimping for staff salaries?" I ask.

"Yes," she says.

"At least you know what we're doing here," I say.

"B-roll," she says. "We are doing B-roll followed by bat time editing."

"And the thing we practice now that we do really well will

hopefully have the opportunity for something worthwhile in the future?" I ask.

"Yes," she says.

"Then we forgive our getting better. We forgive this extra day of B-roll," I say. "And do you know what we call video shoots? I mean what we call it on the inside?"

"What you call it?" she asks.

"Long periods of boredom interrupted by waiting," I say.

"It's true," she says.

I place my eye back in the camera and say. "Things on the inside are a lot different than looking in on them from the outside. That's why the inside takes its toll, for the truth it exacts. That's why I go to the inside. It's my job, was my job, to extricate those who can't find the exits. You can only do that from the inside."

"And ceremonies now?" Natasha asks.

"You mean eco-tourism with a plant medicine chaser?" I ask.

"Good one," she says.

"I'm not afraid of that hole," I say. "I can dive down into it."

"What is the hole?" she asks.

"What you carry to the grave," I say.

"That the hole? That what you dive into with plant medicine, what you carry to the grave?" she asks.

"Yes," I say.

"But I will stop thank you," she says.

"I will too," I say. "It is getting hard on my body, especially that part in the beginning when you have to break through thinking you're going to die. My body just can't take it anymore. But I've learned a lot, learned about calming down. It will comfort me later. It will let me help others."

"And this video what will be?" she asks.

"What it's meant to be," I say.

"What it meant to be?" she asks and I say, "Average with flaws."

"Why we do then?" she asks.

"Because it would have been worse if the other guy had done

it. I hate bad work. I hate people who do it and get paid for it and convince other people to let them. They're well poisoners. Now it will be good enough. That was its highest potential. It will have something good for anyone looking for good."

"This is already such nice conversation," she says. "I can't wait for post-production bat time."

"Then see that guy over there? Let's call him Harvey," I tell her. "Go learn from him. He's our Final Cut Pro editor."

"Why call him Harvey?" she asks

"That's his name," I say.

A tall, gangly guy about six foot six with feet still too big for his height has entered the auditorium and is looking around. When he catches my eye he waves with a big smile.

He lopes over like a cross between a deer and a kangaroo. He almost falls on top of us.

"Here's the list," he says, handing me a sheet of paper.

"This is Natasha," I say. "She's a pole dancer, her sister's an anthropologist, but you can't tell them apart. Go over the list with her then I'll come review it with both of you."

"What list?" Natasha asks.

"The remaining B-roll list," I say.

"I get the dailies," Harvey says.

"And he codes them into scenes," I say.

"Try to piece the story together maybe," he says. "You know through what the people are saying in the principal photography?"

"And since Harvey listens closely to what the people are saying in the interview," I say and Harvey says, "I get the idea of the B-roll we should cut to when we edit in the donuts."

"You are both dangerous people," Natasha says.

"We're done here. I have to see the client," I tell Harvey and he turns from me and says, "So, Natasha, let's go over these notes. We'll find a private office somewhere. Let's follow him to the offices."

Krista Charles' office is not big. But she sits in it like a queen and says, "Why don't you like anything about me and what can I do to change your opinion?"

"I like you. I like everyone," I say, sitting down, and, when I look up, she's leaning forward and her big chair is rocking. "So it's true!" she says. "Come on. Teach me to have you like me. This video is important to me."

"To *you*," I say.

"Yes to me and to this organization," she says.

"I get it," I say. "You want me to like you but that's not what you mean. What you mean is you want me to like you on camera."

"What else is there?" she asks.

"There's a world of what else is there," I say and she says, "But if I can't do it for you I can't do it for anyone. You're the one staring at me through the lens. So what can I do to have you like me?"

"You're afraid this isn't going well. But its fine," I say. "If there is always a truth to hide, you want me to make sure that truth stays hidden."

"I want you to like me. Did I dress wrong?" she asks.

"No," I say.

"Then why don't you like me?" she asks.

"Okay, there was one thing you said that was troubling," I say. "I've talked about it behind your back so it really got under my skin. You said be careful driving or one day you may be working for me. You view these people as working for you. How much do you make anyway, six figures? These people are stuffing spice jars all day long into your wallet. That's how you phrased it. That's how it came across on camera. That's your world view. Reframe that and I'll like you. Don't worry. It will die on the cutting room floor anyway. I wouldn't do that to you. But maybe it comes across in other ways and in other places I'm not seeing. Truth metastasizes that way and no one can hide that kind of truth."

"What truth?" she asks.

"Perhaps it's your focus on yourself in general. You come across as a compulsive hedonist," I say, getting up. "I can work around it.

I like your sister. She saved a friend of mine actually."

I'm on my feet now and she says, "You have me wrong. You have this place wrong. How can I prove it to you?" and I push in the chair and say, "I've interviewed your gadget inventors, your patients, your supervisors, your patients' family members, your board members, your donors and your community leaders. You'll be represented well. It will be a good story. I don't see the hook yet, that's all, that one thing that wraps it all up in a phrase that can be used as a title except for the one I can't use that you see these people working for."

"Let me go back on camera," she says.

"Let Harvey film you then," I say. "That way you won't have to look at me."

"And here comes *this* moment!" Harvey says, swiveling around in the editing bay. "She's a pro I tell you."

"People who hate their jobs can still be very good at their jobs," I say.

"Thus the golden strangulation," Harvey says.

On screen, Krista Charles is saying, "If it is true that we only see ourselves then look. This is you. This is you. This is you."

"We cut away here to different patient close-ups tight on faces," Harvey says, hitting pause.

"I get it," I tell him. "She's moved it out. She's moved it away from herself."

"And get this," he says, hitting play, and Krista Charles says, "These people, the wonderful people we work with, are you except for an accident of birth or an accident in life. They're you. And if you see that then appreciate the work we are doing keeping positive."

"Now we bring up music here, barely audible, building slowly, new age, inspiring," Harvey says and Krista Charles says, "- producing products, being valuable to society, maintain pride with a livable wage, attaining independence, making friends, planning for the future. So when you look around and you only see yourself, see yourself here. You can't change the past, but you can help change what happens next."

"Music builds, telephone number begins rising slowly. For more information or to donate or offer support," Harvey says.

"It's okay," I say.

"I told you she was a pro," he says.

"You teach her that *you only see yourself*?" Natasha asks me. "I think I heard before from you."

"I don't remember," I say. "But there. There's the title of the piece."

"You only see yourself?" Natasha asks.

"Staying Positive," I say.

"So can we paste that in as the ending? Maybe use some of the cuts moving across the screen in a mortis?" Harvey asks.

"It's okay," I say. "It's this Elvis bullshit, the crap that saves."

"What is Elvis bullshit?" Natasha asks and I say, "Suckering people into a standing ovation."

"That's Elvis bullshit?" she asks.

"That's what we call it," I say.

"The irony is not to make it as phony as it really is," Harvey says.

"You have to let it be just what it is. Touch it and it reveals, a little push here a little tug there," I say and Natasha suddenly says, "That's why I love you. You explain things to me."

"*I* could explain things to you," Harvey says.

Natasha laughs and falls back on the leather couch. Harvey turns back to the screens and says to his reflection, "That didn't work as planned."

After some manipulation of scenes, he swivels back to Natasha and says, "I worked a whole summer in telephone repair. They gave me assistants to train. I'd show a guy how to do it. Find, identify, connect, connect, connect, and he'd do it. Then we'd go to another location and he'd do it. But in the middle of him doing it, I'd ask why are you doing it? They all said the same thing. What do you mean why? I'd say why does this connect to this and this connect to this, and they had to give me the theory. They had to understand. So here it comes, raise the music, if you know the why, you'll always remember the how. I can explain. I can show you the why."

"Good try," Natasha says and he swivels dejected back to the screens. "Anyway that what Arlo Guthrie told me in Maui. He told me when you know you know," she says.

"Arlo Guthrie?" Harvey asks, beginning to line up the rough cut from the ending back.

"Hana in Maui up the road to Hana," she says.

"So lots of guys explain things to you, but you love this guy for explaining to you," Harvey says.

28

Snap Beans

"I JUST WANT TO THANK YOU," MARVIN THE MOBILE MECHANIC says, coming into the cabin.

"I didn't do anything," I say.

"I know," he says. "Really I know," and Buster lies down at his feet.

"Have you seen the hummingbirds? They're huge," he says. "I was just watering the aloe. They hover there. You should see those hummingbirds right now. They fly in from Mexico. They're bright florescent green."

"What's with you?" I ask and he says, "I'm just in love with your girlfriend, that's all."

"You'll have to accept Jesus as your savior," I tell him.

"I'll accept Elroy the One-Eyed Wonder Snake if it keeps me out of where I'm going," he says.

"The salvation of your soul is what Roxanne cares about," I say.

"And here I thought it could be all about *me*," he says.

"Doctor Dorothy Charles is coming up the hill again. But this time she's coming to see you," I tell him.

"Castrating bitches, I mean theory-driven, pill-pushing hot babes, I like them too, just not as much as Roxanne. That Roxanne is a saint walking among us. But Doctor Dorothy is a smoothed-out Goth, you know, that nasty New York thing all grown up," he says.

He's staring through the closed window when one of those hummingbirds flies up to the glass and hovers right in front of his face.

"Your brother," I say and he turns to me and holds his hand palm up an inch from my face.

"I got *this*," he shouts.

It's a thick black tattoo like a line that crosses the inside of his palm and he says, "I'll always be reaching back to grab the knife that's slitting his throat."

"But your hands are so scarred. No one will notice the tattoo with all the scrapes and burns," I say.

"I'll notice," he says.

"My philosophy exactly," I say and he pulls his hand away from my face.

"I think I'm going for Roxanne even if she is your girlfriend and even if I have to go to church for a while in the beginning, what the hell I'll suffer silently. We'll work it out. Maybe it will be good for me. Maybe I can play my guitar and sing gospel in her church? Do they let you do that in her church? That would be cool. I think I can get into this already. I'm having a full-on change of heart."

"I think Roxanne already found someone," I say.

"Jesus doesn't count as a boyfriend. He's dead," Marvin says.

"He came back," I say.

"I'll compete with Him for her," he says.

"He wins," I say.

"That's a tough kind of winning," he says.

"That's the kind of winning she believes in. You have to die for other people's sins," I say.

"Been there," he says.

"Don't make me give you the whining lecture again," I say.

"That was a good one. I do a good imitation of that one," he says, flopping down on the couch. "Anyway she's a saint. I worship her. She's Zydeco. You know what that means? It means snappy. Actually I think it means snap beans. She's snappy. You can't be better than snappy."

"You can worship someone at a distance and sometimes it can be better that way," I say.

"You saying there's something about her up close?" he asks the ceiling.

"So you don't know?" I ask.

"Know what?" he asks.

"That she's perfect up close," I say.

"What gives you the right to say I don't have a chance?" he asks.

"Just the opposite," I say.

"She's perfect up close, right?" he asks.

"She's even perfect at a distance," I say.

"So you say I don't have a chance," he says.

"Okay, Marvin, stop screwing with me. I'm tired," I say and he says, "Ah, now you're getting smart. It's taken you a while."

"Doctor Charles is coming up the hill to offer you a job. This is your heads up," I say.

"A job?" he asks and straightens up, adjusting an invisible tie.

A breeze almost imperceptible touches the eucalyptuses. Leaves rustle. Dry earth more like dust shifts low on the street. Sumac commences to stink. There's a scurrying movement down in the bushes.

"Steady income," I say. "Take it. Don't blow it."

"What's the gig?" he asks and I say, "She'll tell you."

"That's not much of a heads up," he says and I say, "Just tell me you'll take it and you won't fuck it up by saying no."

Marvin flops back down on the couch. "What would Jesus do?" he asks the ceiling.

Buster walks over to be petted. Marvin drops a hand to his head and he groans. Then he barks and Marvin says, "Car just came in the front gate."

"She's here," I say. "Don't fuck it up."

"Go get her, Buster," he says and soon Dorothy Charles and Buster come in the cabin. I can see what Marvin is talking about. He's right. She's is a Goth girl. The blackish lipstick, black eyeliner, sharp features, red hair, black nail polish, tightly cut nails, she's a smoothed out Goth girl and she's asking, "Did you tell him?"

"Only that you have a job for him," I say.

"One that Jesus would take," Marvin says and she says, "It's a nurse but it's a lot different and you get a scholarship to go back to university and get a nursing degree. You'll work with my out-patients and in-hospital patients the way you work with Big Larry. It's like a social worker but more like an advocate and most like a liaison. You deal with the patients on their levels and bring me their realities."

"You mean psychiatric patients?" Marvin asks.

"Some," she says.

"And I can speak English, direct English?" he asks.

"That's why we need you," she says.

"I guess it beats being under cars," he says.

"Or meth or the morgue," Dorothy Charles says.

"See this tattoo?" he says, shoving it in her face. "Roxanne suggested it. I can show it to myself and say a prayer right through it. Or I can point it somewhere."

"Why don't you show her your florescent hummingbirds?" I suggest.

"Is that a euphemism?" Dorothy Charles asks.

"Follow me," Marvin says. "There are hummingbirds that fly up from Mexico and they're in the front garden right now. Watch this," he says, turning on the sprinkler, and the humming birds appear.

"Oh my," Dorothy Charles says.

"Do you know what they're doing? They're celebrating because I'm taking this job," he tells her.

"What is it about this street and this tiny little town?" she asks me and she turns to Marvin and says, "Bring this with you."

"Bring what?" he asks.

"This street," she says.

"I'll bring this street wherever you want," Marvin says. "But streets can be long and one end might not be like the other end."

"Bring this end," Dorothy Charles says and Marvin says, "Zydeco!" and she asks, "What does that mean?" and he says, "It means snappy. It means yes. It means beans. You're Zydeco, Doctor Dorothy."

"Beans means yes?" she asks.

"I've decided to celebrate with Roxanne tonight," Marvin says. "I'm calling her right now at the courthouse. We'll have clam chowder at the Brigantine, the one down near San Diego State not that crappy one up by the Del Mar racetrack. That's what I'm suggesting, that we all go there, except I don't really like clam chowder."

"He's after my girlfriend," I tell Dorothy Charles.

"Then I'll go with *you* so it can be a double date," she says.

"Suggest She's Okay," I tell Marvin.

"She's Okay?" he asks.

"It's not She's Okay. It's a Japanese Restaurant that just sounds like She's Okay. It has great bento boxes and it's down by San Diego State in La Mesa and Roxanne likes it there," I say.

When we get there, Marvin tells Roxanne, "I picked up these two barnacles. But I just want to be alone with you."

"We came along to protect you," Dorothy Charles says.

"You mean protect Marvin," Roxanne laughs.

"I knew this was a bad idea," he says. "I want you to be my

girlfriend. I'll do whatever it takes."

"Church," I say.

"This Sunday," Marvin says.

"Bento Box," Roxanne says to the waitress.

"The one with the gyozas," I say.

"I just accepted a job at the hospital," Marvin tells her. "See this tattoo?" and he holds it up to Roxanne's face.

"Oh, that looks so good. They did a nice job!" she tells him. "Now you can't keep living at your aunt's house with all those wrecked cars. That's where you've been staying, right?"

"Not anymore," he says. "I'm moving in with you."

"Maybe I can talk to my minister about a place for you to stay," Roxanne says and Marvin turns to me and says, "I told you church would be cool!"

Dorothy Charles raises her water glass and says, "This is a celebration. To Marvin and all the good he will do in his new job. We really need you, Marvin."

"How can you start work without training?" Roxanne asks and Dorothy Charles says, "It's on the job training like an intern. Do you know how hospitals are structured these days? There's the hospital with its facilities and staff. There are also private practices inside the hospital paying the hospital rent. I and several doctors have one of these private practices inside the hospital. He used to have one too," she says, touching my shoulder. "I can hire anyone. If one of my patients needs to stay in the hospital or needs an operation, that patient gets three bills. One is from the hospital. One is from my practice. And one is from some other practice like an anesthesiologist. I don't need to release my patients to the hospital. I can do everything inside my own practice except operations. Then the patient only gets my bill. I pay the hospital rent."

"So you hired Marvin," Roxanne says.

"Yes," Dorothy Charles says.

"You got a good man," she says, raising her water glass again.

"Excuse me," Marvin says to the waitress, "Do you have frog's legs? Then hop over there and bring us our Bento boxes," then he turns to Roxanne and asks, "If I called you to meet me alone somewhere, would you come?" and she says, "If I needed my car fixed."

"I knew a guy who left instructions to have his cremated ashes sprinkled over his former girlfriend's head. I didn't do it," Marvin says. "I was there though. We rang her doorbell. When she stepped outside, it's not like sand either, there are boney clumps. It depends how fat you are I guess in the oven or something."

"What did she do?" Roxanne asks.

"When we told her what it was. I mean, who it was," Marvin says, "she just dropped her head with all that stuff all over her. She didn't yell at us or close the door or anything. She just dropped her head and stood there in the doorway. The funny thing is we lost our anger. We stood there with her. It was a solemn moment. I don't know why I remembered that. I think we're good friends here at this table. I could see why my friend loved her."

"Tap three times on the table means thank-you," Roxanne says. "Look down when you tap. Don't look at the emperor's face. Go tap-tap-tap."

"You can't trust people who can't live alone or who want to. My husband is like that," Dorothy Charles says.

"Which way is he?" Marvin asks.

"Oh-oh, Marvin's on the prowl again. Hey, Marvin, I thought you were after me?" Roxanne says.

"But you just want things fixed," he says.

"So do *I*," Dorothy Charles says.

"Here's the bento boxes," Roxanne says.

"Drop your heads. Tap three times," Marvin says.

29

Yellow Bird

"SUISEKI," NATASHA SAYS. "IT'S THE ART OF LOOKING AT ROCKS. We have rocks all over our house now."

"Oh, you guys live together?" Harvey asks.

"With my sister too," Natasha tells him.

"You live with two women?" he asks me.

"Twins," I say.

"Twins like another one of her?" he asks.

"Can't tell them apart," I say.

"He can," Natasha says.

"I'm sick," Harvey says.

He stretches in the chair.

"The rough cut is done," he says. "That was a brutal ten hours of editing.

Natasha stands. I stand. Harvey stands.

"We walk up rivers," Natasha tells him. "We collect rocks that call to us. We find feathers. We dance and drum. We have so much fun here in Pacific Northwest."

"So now ceremony is okay?" I ask and Harvey turns at the door and points back into the room saying, "And look at this place. Freeze frame this is where I spend my life. It's room after room like this. They're all the same. They may as well all be the same room. I have a room like this in my *house*. Freeze frame no windows, freeze frame grey walls, freeze frame small round ceiling lights, freeze frame black leather couch, freeze frame three Herman Miller chairs, freeze frame desk, freeze frame computer, freeze frame double monitors. Get me outdoors. Some editors have pictures of Grizzlies and Denali National Park on their walls. But they never leave their rooms."

"You must come with us. We take you places," Natasha tells him. "We get rocks and feathers together."

"I knew this would work if I stayed at it," Harvey tells her.

"We let you do ceremony," Natasha says and Harvey turns off the lights. In the hallway she says, "Then you will be happy in editing room. Indian ceremony all about pain and boredom, you spend night on hard ground then you sore and crunched over in morning. You lose old complaint. You have new complaint. You go back to things you dislike and now you like. On way back maybe find a feather or a rock."

"I'm in," Harvey says. "I'm good with pain and boredom."

"But you need tuck long legs. Lots of people sit around circle. Not good skinny guy size twelve shoes take too much space," she says.

"I'll be space-less," he says and she says, "You think funny now. Wait until you really space-less in place of silence. You get thoughts you not ask for."

"I just got one of those thoughts right now," he says.

"Where we go eat? I'm hungry," she says.

We drive along 156th Avenue in Bellevue past Saint Louise de Marillac Catholic Church and all its outbuildings.

"We are all one body," Natasha says, reading the sign, and

Harvey says, "Maybe there's a good rock in their parking lot, a rock that will call to me. Maybe there's a feather from a crow."

"Maybe better one at Crossroads," Natasha says. "I like this area. It is so strange around Crossroads Shopping Center. We see lots of Russians there and Muslims. I buy book at secondhand bookstore about Django Reinhardt and badly burned two fingers. We watch men play chess with four foot chess pieces. They like me there."

"I'm sure they do," Harvey says.

"But we not go there. We pass Crossroads Shopping Center. This crazy area so much here but can't find if not already know. Uwajimaya sometimes good prices on Fuji apples but it moved location. Top Foods good for Bavarian rye. We go Café Ori local knowledge big surprise for you in Ross Dress-for-Less Plaza. They like me there."

"I'm sure they do," Harvey says again. "I'm hungry. What do they serve?"

"Everything in world," Natasha says, pointing him down to the menu under the table glass.

"Mine's all in Chinese," he says. "It's like computer code. You can't decipher human intent from computer code."

"So look here," she says, pointing at the next menu under the glass.

"Do they like you there too? Under the glass?" he asks. "You know, the air of fact enhanced through repetition."

"If I don't like you, that's okay right?" Natasha asks.

"Now you've taken your life in your hands," I tell him.

"I'm an editor," Harvey says. "My life is always in my hands."

"Not like this," I tell him.

"I'm just so damn attracted to you. What can I teach you, please?" he asks and Natasha stares at the menu without looking up. "Everyone want teach me," she says.

"But I know Final Cut Pro," he says.

"I not make sex deals with insulting person," she says.

"Lose your appetite yet, Harvey?" I ask.

There are one hundred and seventy-five items on the Café Ori menu divided into sections. These are appetizers, soup, curry, seafood, beef/pork, chicken, hot pot, bean curd, vegetables, rice/spaghetti, fried noodle, soup noodle, congee, Taiwanese shaved ice and drinks. Numbered items are in each section starting in appetizers with 1: French toast then ending in drinks with 175: water melon pearl.

"No credit cards at Café Ori," Natasha says.

"Some people still like the feel of cash," I say.

"Not me!" Natasha says. "I hate the feel of cash. Money it make you sick. Germ is like little syringe. You touch paper, plunger squeeze sick into you."

"I'm in love," Harvey says.

"In love not help you," Natasha says.

I look down and tap my fingers three times on the table.

"What's that?" Harvey asks.

"Don't look at the emperor's face," I say.

Harvey starts to sing.

"Knock three times on the ceiling if you want me, mmm-hmmm, twice on the pipe if the answer is no-oh."

"Where pipe?" Natasha asks.

There are only a few people in the restaurant, a family and three couples, all Asian. It's night. Although Café Ori has doubled in size, it's because of all the Microsoft lunch business. We are at the table-for-four by the faux fireplace and the Southwestern painting of the Indian on an Appaloosa. There is a high counter in front of the kitchen and our waitress comes around to refill our glasses of tea. Harvey is now shoveling food into his mouth, the Number 30 Sauteed Rock Cod Fillet, the Number 50 Portuguese Chicken and the Number 129 Black Bean Sparerib Chow Fun. He even makes his way back to Number 8 Hot and Sour Soup.

"Now maybe I like you," Natasha says. "A man with such appetite."

"And here I thought you rang a bell you can't un-ring," I say.

"No that was you," Marvin says.

"Marvin, did you see the tattoo I got? It's the one on your hand," I say.

"What you thinking?" Natasha asks and I say, "When I first moved here and the trees were against the house. Remember when they slammed against the roof when the wind blew? It was just before you took them down with the chainsaw. Maybe it was just before winter. There was a yellow bird. Remember that yellow bird?"

"When you were with my sister before I move in too?" she asks.

"What?" Harvey asks.

"You were there," I say. "Remember the yellow bird that kept tapping on our window? That was so glorious. Do you remember that?"

"Maybe that was in San Diego," she says.

"It was here, a yellow bird tapping," I say.

"Three times," Roxanne says.

"Is this how we work on video?" Natasha asks.

30

Rancho Santa Fe

RANCHO SANTA FE RISES IN THE EAST UP FROM SOLANA BEACH along Via de La Valle like a Eucalyptus mountain forest in the San Diego sun. It rises from desire to accomplishment, from intelligence to knowledge and from guessing to knowing. There's new money and old money. New money built the large, tasteless mausoleums-to-my-masculinities and old money built the lovely haciendas and happy little horse ranches. But it's all money, all buying power, all shopping power and all power. I'm in the process of buying a house here.

"Don't you want this?" I say to my wife and she doesn't answer again.

"Isn't it exciting?" I say. "Sanders and his Mexican crew can plant an orchard on the acreage. They can manage it too and Tom and his wife will design a purple swimming pool shaped like a bass guitar for you. You can look out and see oranges and lemons all year round. It will be like Christmas all the time and they'll look like Christmas trees full of Christmas bulbs."

She's sitting on the far side of the front seat. She's jammed against the door as if she can't get farther away. We're riding in the black lacquer 1966 Cadillac de Ville convertible, my latest ground-up restoration, this one with the wide whitewalls I bought from New Zealand. The top is down, always down, although I like the hooks to secure it up. I like the look of the hooks and how they feel and how the mechanisms move. My wife is wearing a pink sweatshirt with a picture of a finger pointing left above the words I'M WITH STUPID. She's looking away but it's impossible to tell where she's looking. Her head is down as if she's looking at the weeds just off the side of the road.

There are other roads into Rancho Santa Fe besides the Via de La Valle road. The back road into Rancho Santa Fe, if you live west and north, runs over the top of La Costa along Rancho Santa Fe Road down through the narrow community of Olivenhain. That's where we're driving. Those are the weeds she's looking at. As we turn left onto El Camino Del Norte, a woman going the other way mouths, "Nice car!"

For some reason that mouthing dawns on me that this is near the end. I can't consider her my wife anymore. We're faking a beginning. I am. She's not. Driving is like that. Goodwill tries to imbed even in the darkest hours. "It's been building all day," I say, but again she doesn't respond. That was a weak attempt on my part. You can't close the deal if you can't breach the subject. "All I want is an indication that you want this house," I say.

"Whatever you want, Darling," she finally says under her breath.

I don't realize she's drunk until we get to the house and she won't leave the car. She's thinking about the mechanics of walking to the house, but she can't get past the thinking of the mechanics. I've seen it before. But this time is different. There's nothing left. I don't understand a person who pulls unhappiness from each thrilling moment, who tags failure to every success, and who can't find pleasure in achievement or environment. Maybe she'll be happy with someone else. I am. I'm in love with Swims with Horses, but I still want this house. I want Rancho Santa Fe. I want my family because that's the gate through which this eventuality is flowing. I only think about the word, the actual word, divorce, when I knock on the front door and a gorgeous woman with dark eyes opens it.

"We never thought we'd get it. We're so happy," she says.

She has a paint roller in her hand.

I stare into her eyes. She's smart and honest.

"It's a wonderful house," I say. "My wife and I were thinking of, well, we made an offer. We've been driving up here every few days, I mean, to think about making the counter offer."

"Well we're so happy," she says again and I just turn away, get in the car, start it, back out of the driveway and head up the street. We drive through Rancho Santa Fe. The names are so lovely. Los Morros, Ramble de Las Flores, Lago Lindo, Senda de la Luna, Linea del Cielo, El Secreto. I have my secret. We drive east.

We're out of Rancho Santa Fe now and driving along the Del Dios Highway. All changes here. Healing dies in general and in specific. I look at my wife then beyond her up the steep canyons. Soon the canyons narrow and give way to the dam that forms Lake Hodges. I was here two days ago with Swims with Horses.

I'm humping Swims with Horses from behind with our clothes on. We're on the shore. She's bending over and looking at the lake. Moments ago we were walking along and talking when out of pure love I started rubbing on her. Now a hiker farther down the shore approaches until he sees what we're doing and takes an immediate right away from the water. He just disappears. I close my eyes. I can't believe what I'm feeling. I don't know how long I've been feeling this way. I ejaculate in my pants. All that tension digitizes like the sparkles on the lake.

"I came in my pants," I say.

"I did too," she says. "I come when you come. That's how I was taught."

I don't mention the guy who walked off the shore. We're not saying anything. I love her silence. I love her conversations.

She says, "I was in the bathroom at work reading a book where a girl goes into a bathroom to commit suicide. It was a crazy day. It started when I was in a meeting with our director and I realized I'd forgotten to put on makeup this morning so I smiled a lot. I have to fly to Colorado tomorrow for the company training I told you about."

"But I thought we were going together," I say. "I thought we agreed that you'd tell me when it was and I'd get a ticket."

She's facing me now.

She says," My husband said he wants to go. So what could I do?"

"We're at a critical juncture," I say. "How many critical junctures do people have in a lifetimes? This is ours."

She's in Colorado now and I'm here driving around Lake Hodges. The sun sparkles off the ripples and I know why I drove here. It was as if I was magnetized to drive here.

"My teeth are breaking," I say to my wife. I hold out a piece of enamel. She turns to look at it.

I say, "First one tooth cracked then a second tooth cracked. Look at this one. My teeth are breaking."

31

Wandering Healer

"Hi, how's it going?"

"Who are you?"

"I'm the wandering healer. I get paid to sit with people in the corridor and annoy them in their moment of crisis."

"They let dogs in here?"

"Buster goes where I go. What happened to your wrists?"

"I tried to commit suicide over a boy. Happy?"

"I wish someone would do that for me. There's this girl I really like, my therapist's girlfriend, and he's leaving town even though my brother just got murdered, and his girlfriend isn't really into me let alone slitting her wrists for me. You didn't do it right, you know."

"Didn't do what right?"

"You need to slit the razor upwards not across if you really want to do damage. What did he do to you anyway?"

"None of your business even if you think it is."

"Then tell Buster. I'll listen to my iPod. Tap me on the shoulder when you're done explaining to Buster. Ah, Bob Wills and the Texas Playboys. Dance all night, dance a little longer, throw off your coat, throw it in the corner; don't see why you don't stay a little longer."

"You're weird."

"What?"

"I said you're weird!"

"Done explaining yourself to Buster? Stay all night, stay a little longer, don't see why you don't stay a little longer."

"Yes, I'm done explaining. Stop singing and stop dancing."

"Am I embarrassing you? You're the one with the wrists. Here, want to listen?"

"No."

"I see your mean side, you know. I test for it all the time with people right from the start. I'm relentless at testing, if you must know. There it is again. That stare is pretty mean. I'm just kidding. I don't see it. Actually you pass."

"I like Buster."

"He likes you. I like you too, if you must know, but not as much as my therapist's girlfriend who soon isn't going to be his girlfriend when he moves to Seattle. Then she'll marry some other guy and someone else will have to help me. There was another Buster once, but he got struck by a rattler."

"Maybe I can help you."

"Only if you're over your boyfriend and I mean it. I don't want someone helping me carrying around dead weight. Pretty soon it becomes my dead weight. You know how that works. Nobody's that strong to get helped by a taker."

"I'm not a taker."

"I noticed that about you from the start. Want to see my tattoo?"

32

Mister Happy Face Is Dead

"YOU'RE SO SWEET. THAT'S SUCH A NICE THING TO SAY. DID I make A mistake back then?" Swims with Horses asks.

"Of course you did. But don't be sad. We're here now," I say.

"Remember I fell off that horse in Colorado when I was there for corporate training? I got a head injury. I even threw up which is a sign of head trauma. I wasn't in full command of my senses when I got back to San Diego," she says.

"Oh, no, it's a dream," I mutter. I knew it. It's a dream. It's a good dream though, not the usual nightmare where she never speaks to me or is surrounded by people and I can't get close to her. Worst of all are those visits to Issaquah where I can't even find her. I roll over. It's a dream and I'm still partly in it. "At least she spoke," I mutter. We said things to each other. We got to a point of understanding. It was in the present.

Natasha has one long leg out from under the covers.

"You look happy," she says to me.

"I wasn't visiting Issaquah," I say.

"That remind me I must shop at Costco today," she says and Julia walks into the bedroom bone naked holding a mug of coffee. She sinks into the over-stuffed green chair and crosses her legs.

"We need eggs, pecans and albacore in water, Chicken of the Sea brand," she says.

I float into being awake again.

Natasha is staring at me.

She says, "If I run someday, you will have to chase me."

Julia looks past us out the window to the cascades.

"Lots of snow," she says.

"We deliver video today," Natasha says, walking in front of her toward the bathroom. "We review for final time. It is final preview, then we bring to client. See I learn production language."

"Faculty meeting today," Julia says. "University deans on big push find new students, especially dean for continuing education. All of a sudden he must compete with Community Colleges."

"Maybe Warren-" I begin to say and she says, "No talk Warren."

"September and October gone now really autumn, deep autumn," Natasha says, turning on the shower.

I follow Julia's stare. She's right. Everything is gold and green in the valley below our perch, but there's snow on the mountains.

I say. "November rings a bell that can't be un-rung. There's no turning back now."

"This year big winter," Julia says. "You never meet perfect people in winter only in spring and summer. What we do is with head down in winter. In spring and summer we are head up. We do what we don't know. Then we find perfect people, like how we find you."

At Café Ori this afternoon it's the Number 27 Sautéed Fish with Crème of Corn, the Number 74 Hai Nan Chicken Rice and the Number 138 Shredded Pork with Preserved Vegetables Soup Noodle. Harvey turns his laptop then moves his chair so he can see it too.

He says, "I can't stand this weather. It won't be sunny for months. I'll be crazy. I'm already crazy. Can't we get a gig down in New Mexico or someplace? Hey, how about San Diego? Here, watch this, here it comes. This is the part I tweaked. Check it out. It took a while to render."

Dr. Krista Charles on screen finishes her speech and the box that contains her slowly becomes smaller and fades out as other scenes in boxes push across the screen from left and right and up and down. The music rises. All scene boxes fade out. The name of the institution and the telephone number takes center screen with the words You Can Help. We Can Provide.

"I think I'll puke now," I say and Harvey says to Natasha, "That means he likes it."

Café Ori is packed and steamy, but we're the only table with a computer on. Now Harvey closes it.

"Come on admit it. It works," he says.

"I like," Natasha says.

"That's good," I say, "because you're presenting it to Doctor Charles."

"Me? Why me?" she asks and Harvey already has his head down in the Number 138 Shredded Pork with Preserved Vegetables Soup Noodle. He slurps up a mouthful and starts giggling. He chokes a bit, regains himself, and says, "Because she doesn't like you because you're hot."

"That true?" Natasha asks me and I give the shrug that's a nod.

Then Harvey says, "If the video keeps together through her dislike of you, it's good."

"So I am test?" Natasha asks.

"We have to have *some* fun," Harvey says and she says, "So next time we find someone who not like you. Not so hard to find I think."

"Okay with me as long as next time you learn how to mortise with Final Cut Pro," he says.

"I want to learn that," Natasha says.

"This is all coming my way!" Harvey says, punching the air.

An hour later Natasha is presenting in the conference room.

"So we make presentation for fundraising effort," she's saying in front of the big screen, "but also for general public and new employees to learn about this place and good work it does."

Krista Charles sits back with her arms crossed. Several of her Board members are in the room. She stares a hole in me. Natasha signals Harvey to play the video. She steps aside and the opening segment appears with a blast of music. Eight and a half minutes later the room bursts into applause. Nobody stands to leave and nobody talks. Everyone waits for the alpha to self-reveal.

"I knew they'd be happy, damn this weather," Harvey says back in the car. "Believe me I knew. Donors like to cry. There was no way to jinx this job. That guy, the wide body next to her, who was he? The one who asked which one of us came up with you can help, we can provide?"

"Microsoft Vice President," I say.

"Oh yes?" Natasha asks.

"How did you like what he said?" Harvey says. "We need to put that on all our materials! I told you it was a good line."

"It's all you, Harvey," I say.

"We pulled it off," he says.

The Explorer rolls onto the 520 bridge.

Natasha says, "Doctor Krista is happy. Big Microsoft guy say good job to her. Now we stream video off website and place link in monthly newsletters. We post on social networking sites. We do big awareness marketing push. I learn. I thank you both so much."

Harvey says, "The sheer act of doing gives you inner peace."

"I can learn more. You will see," Natasha says.

"We need clients," Harvey says.

"Clients will show up now. I've seen it before," I say.

"Maybe we work Microsoft?" Natasha asks.

"I hate training videos," I say.

"But a friend of mine has a vendor number. We can go through his company and he'll only take fifteen percent," Harvey says.

"What is vendor number?" she asks.

"Permission to steal," he tells her. "And Microsoft is making a push into the medical field. That's your gig right, Doctor Hospital Video Director Producer?" he says to me. "I can find the money. My friend can. He knows where to look and that's everything. It's being spent right now. We need to get that money before everything shuts down prior to Christmas. Let's get that wide-body board member as our mole."

"Harvey, you not mind weather all of sudden," Natasha says.

"God it sucks. Low brooding sky thanks for reminding me," he says. "But money eases agony. That's what money does. That's what it's for."

"Is Mister Happy Face dead?" Natasha asks. "We let you out now. There's your car."

"That's a good slogan," Harvey says. "Maybe we'll use it as a stinger on the next project? Mister Happy Face Is Dead. You Can Help. We Can Provide. Call 1-800-nolo-contendo." He gets out of the car and sticks his head back in. "Remember, Natasha baby, you can only jinx something true. We stomped all over this one, Elvis ending and the whole mortise-music-climax bit. We tried to jinx it but there was no jinxing it. Do you know why? You can only jinx truth. And the few times we face truth we just let it be what it is. In fact we live to not touch up something because it feels so good just how it is. For future reference, baby, if we eat *before*, it's as good as it can be for what it is. If we eat *after*, it's to celebrate truth. There's an ugly winter coming. Heavy snow up where you are. It will probably just suck slush down here in Bellevue. Adios."

33

Bungalows

NOBODY NEEDS TO TELL ANYONE IN SAN DIEGO THAT ITS winter. Surfers drift off beaches no reason to be there and the homeless pour closer to the water's edge. All outdoor playgrounds seem out of bounds. Visitors think they've arrived in summer, but if you live here you feel the mean low sixties, the harsh fifties and sometimes at night even the brutal forties and you have to turn on the furnace or the heater. You wear the wrong clothes. It's all a false claim like a bad advertising campaign. Maybe it's the sun you can see but can't feel. You just know you're in a place that's lying to you. Avocado trees die. Frost kills.

Roxanne and I are rollerblading through La Jolla on the hills down toward Bird Rock. The streets are empty. It's between Christmas and New Year. The mansions look cold and solitary. Roxanne is in a red jacket with red tights and red socks and a big button that reads Jesus is the Reason for the Season. She's been wearing that button for weeks. Her smile is radiant. We skate down the middle of the streets. There are no cars.

"This is the busiest time of the year on the psych ward," I tell her and she breaks into laughter.

"No really it's true. Winter makes people crazy," I say.

"What winter?" she laughs, spreading her arms to say look around.

"Celebration pushes people over the edge," I say. "They can't break the loneliness cycle."

"They can find Jesus," she says. "They can be grateful. They can heal."

"Or they can heal by skating with the Zamboners," I say.

The empty road swerves and we get a full view of the California coast.

I say, "The Zamboners played a few floor hockey games at an outdoor rink off El Cajon Boulevard. Now there's a brutal sport. You play on concrete in your running shoes. That means everyone is as fast as anyone else, so lousy players and goons can keep up with you. I don't know who talked us into it. Someone always went to the hospital. I took four stiches right over my eye and played the rest of the game with a bandana tied over it and those guys were still swinging at me."

"I wish I would have seen you guys," Roxanne says.

"We had a lot of passion, the kind that makes you not know you're crazy," I say. "El Cajon Boulevard is a real toilet holster. I'm at the urinal at the rink that night I got injured. A gorgeous woman with lipstick, red fingernail polish and long black hair steps up to the urinal next to me and commences to urinate. It's this little guy dressed like a chick and he does his business and disappears into the scuzzy park next to the rink. There's passion. He's out to trick some guy into getting it on with him. He'll get murdered. I remember thinking here I am with my play passion and here's this guy putting it all on the line for his life passion."

"What do you expect on El Cajon Boulevard?" she asks.

"I'm just saying that life doesn't let hot blood off easy," I say. "It was near that place that sells chicken pot pies. Seniors flock there."

"Transvestite hookers and seniors, El Cajon Boulevard," she says and the road swerves away from the ocean into bungalows built in the mid-sixties. Some places just stop you. Without motioning or speaking, we just head back the other way.

A block away, I say, "Those bungalows felt like death. I didn't know it until now. I'm dropping the word bungalow into my vocabulary."

Roxanne says, "I heard an interview with Maya Lin, the designer of the Viet Nam Memorial. She said something like you keep being the sum total of everything you've ever known and everything you've ever done until one day it percolates up and you wake up and know just what you want to do. I like listening to artists talk. That's how it was for me. One day I woke up and there was Jesus in my life forever."

"See over there, that's where a guy dumped garbage on me," I say.

"Why did he do that?" she asks.

"Because I was wearing white rollerblades and he thought I was a homosexual," I say.

"How do you know that?" she asks.

"Because he yelled homo then dumped garbage out of his car window on me," I say.

"He got that wrong," she says.

"He got more than that wrong," I say.

"What would you do if you saw him right now?" she asks and I say, "Laugh my ass off at him again."

"Oh-oh, I think the Zamboner is surfacing. Let's skate up there and get an Americano," she says, pointing up the street at a café.

"That's a good idea," I say.

We're sitting outside at the café, watching nothing going past in La Jolla. The wind blows off the shores and I suddenly feel chilled from the sweat inside my T-shirt.

"Are you cold? I'll get lids and we can go. I don't think you're moving to Seattle. You'll get too cold," she says.

When she returns with the lids, I say, "Sometimes in therapy my job is to stand quite still and not give the man-group hug especially when it feels like it's a man-group hug moment. That's definitely not the time for a man-group hug."

"Maybe you *are* a homo," she says.

"I was talking about Marvin at the morgue," I say.

"I hugged him," she says, sitting down again.

"Well you're the man-group hugger," I say.

"Would you have hugged him if I wasn't there?" she asks and I say, "No. That's the moment to give space. That's what I'm talking about professionally. When the connection is complete, a demonstration of its completeness is a diluter. It can turn into... bungalows."

"What the-" she asks.

"Never mind," I say. "I was trying it out. It didn't work."

"Bungalows," she says.

"See... right now... man-group hug... not good," I say and she snaps the lid on my Americano and says, "Let's go."

"But I was right," I say as we head down Prospect. "Don't pat your dog while it's eating."

"Don't what?' she asks.

"Don't break the connection by acknowledging it," I say.

"I wonder how Marvin is doing at the hospital with it being so busy right now?" she asks. "Get me some turtle soup and make it snappy. I love *all* that stuff. I love all your friends."

"They're clients actually, non-paying clients. Marvin gets you. He understands what you're all about. He's willing to accept Jesus for you," I say.

"And that's a good enough reason?" she asks.

"He fixed my Avanti. You must admit that's about as impressive as it gets," I say, and we turn a corner and approach her Ford Ranger.

"Oh, look where we are. Hold my cup," she says. "What a lovely time."

34

The Womb of the Chant

ALL IS WHITE. WE'VE BEEN SNOWED IN FOR THREE DAYS. THE generator barks and hums behind the house. Deer tracks crisscross the snow. Mount Si disappears and appears. The fire is crackling in the stone fireplace. Nudity abounds.

"We live like this forever," Natasha says, turning up the Bose speakers.

"Someone comes," Julia says.

"I don't think so," Natasha says.

"I saw something," Julia says.

"What you see?" Natasha asks

"A shape something moves," Julia says.

"Maybe is deer," Natasha says. "I go outside and see maybe with antlers my favorite," Natasha says.

"Like Tundra like wolf or coyote gone now," Julia says.

"But I go outside and look anyway," Natasha says, walking to the leaded glass windows.

I catch her nude reflection in the glass with Julia's nudity superimposed from the couch.

"I see nothing. I go outside now," Natasha says.

"Like that?" I ask and she says, "It will feel good. It will be fun. I will get tingly. I look. I see," and she opens the door and steps into a gust of wind.

I can see that the snow is knee-deep at the front door with Natasha's footsteps breaking through the drift.

Julia closes the door.

"Cold," she says and I walk to the leaded glass windows.

The wind is blowing. The sky is white. Natasha is running around what used to be a driveway. She's making circles and laughing at the tracks she's making. I climb the stairs and get a towel from the bathroom. When I walk down the stairs again, Natasha still hasn't come into the house.

"Soon she dies," Julia says matter-of-factly, looking down at her book and flipping a page.

I step outside and don't see her this time. She's not in the driveway. I look uphill and west. She's running across the garden, kicking up snow and flailing her arms. I take the towel and go back inside the house.

"She's having a ball," I say and Julia still without lifting her head says, "She like outdoor nude. I like indoor nude. Why you not get her? You think let things play out all the time?"

"I thought I'd go draw a bath for her instead," I say.

"Oh you are best man," Julia says and soon the front door blasts open and Natasha rushes in blue, laughing and stomping, and I wrap her in the towel and say, "There's a hot bath for you upstairs."

"Oh you are best man," she says and I say, "That's what your sister said."

"Not Tundra. Not Warren," she says to Julia.

Of course not," Julia says, "Warren in Amazon for one month with Phil McPherson, Tundra with Frank Sid in Port Angeles."

"In Amazon?" Natasha asks.

Julia says, "Warren will fly home in three weeks with ayahuasca for ceremony. It will be invitation only, no university faculty. It is strong medicine, not recreational."

"He change mind. You see. Dean die and you lose job. You go on trial for murder. Okay with me I laugh to see you in jump suit. I take bath now," Natasha says and walks off.

Julia looks up at me and says, "I put clothes on now. Then I go see what I saw outside."

I'm placing alder and cherry on the fire when she walks back downstairs as if out of an L. L. Bean catalog.

"Remember when you move here," she asks, "and we dance around boxes?"

"I remember," I say.

"I am anthropologist. I respect Warren for interest in plant medicines," she says. "Maybe when fly back he different, don't know yet. If he too smart let him swallow plants straighten him out quick. But he is sharing person. Everyone must find way make money. Believe me plant medicine not make much money. Maybe not make any money. Warren give all money he make at Long Dance to follow Phil McPherson to shaman in Peru. He told me. He want be apprentice-shaman learning ways of teacher plant. He must spend full year in jungle someday. You come with me outside? I'm not naked you not need run after me."

Julia and I climb through the snow on the steep hill behind the house. The snow is deep and pushes against our thighs. I say, "The thing with plant medicine is it's hard to take. I thought I was going to die when we did mushrooms. I couldn't breathe. My heart was pounding and not just for a few minutes. I felt like a drowning swimmer and right at the moment of death I broke through."

"Tea," Julia says. "You thought it was tea ceremony."

"And that San Pedro cactus," I say. "I don't know what would have happened to my body if it wasn't dancing and drumming for ten hours?"

"But you learned," Julia says.

"I think I'm gaining an understanding why I'm here," I say.

"And learning that not worth dying for?" she asks.

"Why die to learn why you're here?" I ask. "You understand how crazy your logic is?"

"I am academic. My logic not need be right. I have rubrics," she says.

"So you're willing to die for a clue about why we're here? But the best time in life is when you don't have a clue why we're here. It's called childhood," I say.

"You have such good childhood?" she asks.

"Yes," I say.

"Good for you," she says.

We reach the top of the hill and drop to our knees so the snow is at our necks and we shovel a berm and drop into it. We stare down at the house and the white sky.

Julia says, "Ayahuasca different. Warren explain it this way real medicine. Warren say more serious than all other medicine."

"Are you talking me into things?" I ask.

"I want you there for me," she says.

"And if I'm done with ceremony?" I ask.

"We only ever do a couple. Always we do together. Nothing bad happen when you there. My sister convincing you is no good?" she says and I say, "Maybe your sister is right. You always have to leave a little room for others being right."

"Maybe she is right for her," she says. "Maybe you can be right for you."

I say, "Anyway, I don't want to die like an anthropologist."

"What way that?" she asks and I say, "With dirty fingernails."

"We not always dig," she says.

"I just want to die peacefully in my sleep like my grandfather, not moaning and groaning like his passengers," I say.

"That funny one where you get that?" she asks and I say,

"Marvin the Mobile Mechanic where else."

"That guy," she says. "So you think anthropologists are like passengers."

"Yes," I say.

"Look so beautiful down by house," she says. "I have idea. We can dance around boxes like before. Maybe you kill my sister for us and we live together happy like in beginning? Nobody will know. I will play both parts," and she falls back laughing.

"When did you get a sense of humor?" I ask and she says, "My sister happy, I happy. She saw so much in Russia and even here so much. Now she happy and I thank you. You give her so much. You teach her skills for money. You pour your love into her."

"Me?" I ask.

"You," Marvin the Mobile Mechanic says.

He points a greaseless finger at me and says, "Look around you. You're surrounded by Gods."

We're at Nancy Jane Park, watching Crest on Parade go past. That's what Marvin calls it.

He says, "Look at this. When the people *in* this parade get to the end of the parade, you know at that place behind the general store where that old Mexican gets drunk, they walk back and stand in the crowd to see the rest of the parade. That's why it looks like the number of spectators is growing. But it's just us. It's just the parade watching the parade."

Kids on horseback wearing bicycle helmets pass us followed by kids wearing bicycle helmets on bicycles. Next are the members of the Crest Riding Club wearing sombreros followed by the Crest Garden Club on a flatbed with Gerald the retired General Dynamics engineer driving and farting and with women wearing broad straw hats throwing flowers. Then showing off his new BMW, the jerk-of-the-moment winner, some guy drives two-miles-per-hour with stops and starts over the horse manure. The BMW windows are up for air conditioning reasons and the car is overheating and sputtering and his whole family is inside silently fuming.

"*Prick!*" Marvin yells and everyone looks and laughs. Marvin turns to me. "Better than Disney," he says.

"Look at her," he says, nodding at Roxanne, "There's God walking among us. Ever know a more positive person? She's beautiful and she's kind and she's giving and she's funny and she got me Buster. And this one here," he says at Big Larry. "This is God right here. Nothing can take his humor. Did you ever hear him down on himself? He lost his speech and use of half his body. Did he complain? He's God, I tell you. And this one," he says at Dorothy Charles. "Turn you every which way but loose and she's a medical doctor and she gave me a job doing whatever I do. And this one," he says at Joe. "Did you ever need help and he wasn't there? Plugged toilet, grey water, broken septic, doesn't matter there he is. All he has to do is see you outside for ten minutes screwing up something. Look up he materialized. You're a God magnet. What do you have to say for yourself?"

"Crest on Parade," I say.

"You've got it now," Marvin says.

"F-f-fire engine," Big Larry says, pointing.

"Lot of good it'll do up here with sumac," Marvin says.

"Bad smell," Joe tells Dorothy Charles. "It rises up from down in the canyon. You can smell it for miles. It's almost impossible to describe except if you breathe in hard on a sumac leaf. You can get a hint of it then. It makes you sick. Then add a million plants to that and the burning and the wind and the heat. That's why every twenty years we call it the Crest Fire."

"I h-h-hate sumac," Big Larry says.

"Me too," Joe says.

"That s-smell alone will kill you," Big Larry says.

"First these rodents are all over the place. Then snakes slither to the road and the wind picks up," Joe says.

"These f-firemen on the truck can only wet down a meth house after it explodes," Big Larry says.

"Lucky if they can drive that fire engine out of here when the sumac catches," Joe says. "That's what it's for. It's for escaping."

"See any snakes? Smell any sumac burning?" Marvin asks Dorothy Charles.

"Not today," Roxanne answers. "The jade is plump."

"Spoken like a local," Joe says.

"If we had a brush fire right now, know what I'd do?" Marvin asks.

"H-here it comes," Big Larry says, nudging Roxanne.

"I'd hitch a ride down the hill in that BMW over there with that *prick!*" Marvin yells.

"I think someone needs to get his kids out of that car," Roxanne says.

"The damage is done," I say. "Some lessons you have to ride out. They're in the womb of the chant. It would seem wrong to disturb their agony. It won't end up less of a memory."

"I'm going over there!" Roxanne says and she runs into the parade, bangs on the window, opens the door and pulls out the guy's wife and then his kids.

"That was a mistake," Marvin says.

"I agree," I say.

"Killed my fun," Marvin says.

"Now he s-sits alone in his BMW and *really* knows he's a big prick," Big Larry says.

"There goes your God status," I tell him.

"It's much more fun from here. Stand here," Roxanne says. "But don't listen to him."

"*Me?*" Marvin cries.

"Don't listen to any of them. I'll be back with some watermelon," she says.

Dorothy Charles walks to me and asks, "When are you leaving for Seattle?

"Next month," I tell her.

"Be careful," she says. She pats my chest then grabs it. "Just be careful," she says.

"R-right," Big Larry says. "Sumac doesn't care how plump jade is."

"What you think when look down at such white powerful valley?" Julia asks.

"Sumac and jade," I tell her.

35

Chewing Gum

TODAY IT'S NUMBER 132 PORK CHOP SOUP NOODLE TAIWANESE Style, Number 26 Baked Fish Hong Kong Style, Number 57 Sparerib Hot Pot with Eggplant and Bean Curd, Number 44 Hai Nan Chicken Whole and Number 63 Fried Bean Curd with Salt and Pepper.

Steam flows under Café Ori's kitchen curtain. We're at the big table near the faux fireplace. The Lazy Susan spins dishes around.

"So you just flew up from San Diego yesterday?" Harvey asks Dorothy Charles.

"That's right," she says.

"Ever been here before?" he asks.

"Eight years ago when my sister transferred out from New York," she says.

"The one who runs the clinic, the video we did?" he asks.

"Yes, she's Doctor Krista Charles, a specialist in internal medicine. I'm Doctor Dorothy Charles, a therapist," she says and

Harvey says, "We got so much work off that gig," and Natasha says, "Come on, Harvey, get with program!" then she turns to Dorothy Charles and says, "You his friend?" meaning me, "You know him his whole life when big things happen him in San Diego?"

"I knew him *a* life," Dorothy Charles says. "Maybe I knew him two lives, come to think of it."

"And welcome back, Warren!" Julia says, raising her glass of tea.

"Thank you," Warren says, raising his glass.

"He just fly home now from Amazon where he learned new plant medicine to share with us," Julia tells Dorothy Charles.

"He went with Phil McPherson, another friend," Natasha says to Dorothy Charles then turns to Warren and asks, "So how is Phil McPherson? Since that guy is a dangerous fucking cowboy as you are!"

Dorothy Charles' eyes twinkle.

Natasha says, "Remember dry waterfall with red rocks where Frank Sid got naked and that other guy pass out and Phil McPherson gyrate hands like lightning rod for cosmic energy?"

"Ayahuasqueros don't do that," Warren says.

"So you did ayahuasca in the Amazon? I've heard of ayahuasca," Dorothy Charles says and Warren says, "We brewed it in ceremony down there with a shaman and brought it back in several thermoses. We're having a ceremony tomorrow on the Olympic Peninsula at Frank Sid's house. You're invited."

"Any university people will be there?" Natasha asks.

"Yes," Warren says and Natasha turns to Julia and says, "Told you!"

"I go but not swallow medicine," Julia says. "I will be helper this time."

"And I'll be a helper with you," Warren says.

"I'm curious. I'll go," Dorothy Charles says.

"Then we all go," Julia says and Harvey says, "I'm in. I can go, right? Sounds like a party."

"You'll be puking all night with that attitude," Warren tells him. "Oh and don't eat tomorrow. This is your last meal before tomorrow night's ceremony."

"Then twist that chicken around my way. Look at it outside. This weather sucks," Harvey says, turning the Lazy Susan.

It's definitely blustery outside Café Ori. The rain is part rain and part snow and it's hitting sideways as Dorothy Charles grabs my lapels and pulls me in front of the Video Only store.

"These new people of yours talk like they're mad at each other but they're not are they?" she yells against the wind.

"No," I yell.

"Then what?" she yells.

"That's how we say nothing here in the Pacific Northwest," I yell. "We say the important things quietly."

"But you're the quietest," she yells.

"I have the most to say," I yell.

"Are you living with these women?" she yells.

"Yes," I yell.

"Patients?" she yells.

She pulls me inside the store.

"Maybe you're the patient?" she asks.

"That would be nice," I say.

We turn away from the approaching salesman and incidentally stare at the back of the big screens in the window. There's also a big screen facing us.

I say, "People push against each other up here. But it's more like rubbing than shoving, like a bear against a tree. It's all temperate. Harvey is the newcomer. He needs curing. He's a talented editor, though."

"We don't have much time alone," she says. "Your girlfriends are waiting. It seems you're always in a group. You wanted a clean break from San Diego but you screwed up. You did that video for my sister. It opened a crack in the universe to me. I'll ask you one time about one thing. Wait to answer. Here comes the question.

What happened?"

"She remarried. I haven't seen her," I say.

"You didn't see her?" she asks.

"Pictures on a wall told me the story," I say.

"Sounds like you chanced another restraining order," she says.

"Some gifts are harsher than others," I say. "At least I know what happens to people who get stigmatized. It's not pretty."

"You weren't pretty," Dorothy Charles says.

"But I learned," I say.

"What?" she asks.

"That when you come back to yourself from a place at the absolute far edge of yourself, you come back as a different person. You can say the same words. They don't mean the same things."

"But what happened?" she asks and walks me a couple steps away from the salesman. I can see Julia and Natasha standing by the Explorer.

"It was already a long time ago," I say. "It was when I first moved here. I went to see her."

"We're fine," Dorothy Charles says to the salesman. "We'll look around in a few minutes."

"If you have any questions," he says.

He's chewing gum.

"Thanks," she says.

"I happened to be in the area where she works. I didn't make a trip out of it or anything like that. It wasn't a big plan, just a sudden little pull," I say. "She wasn't there but there were pictures on her office wall. You know what I saw?"

"What?" she asks and I say, "I saw someone else's woman. Not that she's the new guy's woman or anything like that, just someone else's woman. It's like I told Marvin. You have to see that train become a dot down the track and disappear. Then and only then can you let it go because it's long gone."

"Some people move on and some never do," she says. "Actually that's not true. I take it back. Not moving on is moving on too."

"That's a very healthy statement," I say.

"Marvin said something interesting last week. He said nobody gets through life without chasing adversity. He said people confuse neediness with their personalities. Oh yeah, Marvin has a girlfriend."

"We are leaving *now!*" Julia shouts from the car, waving her arms furiously.

"You have *keys!*" Natasha shouts. "Doctor Dorothy, we pick you up tomorrow morning for drive to peninsula!"

We leave Video Only and run sideways against the rain to Dorothy Charles' rental car, and, as she gets in, I yell, "Tell Marvin destra sinistra."

"What's that?" she yells.

"It means right and left in Italian for how to screw Borelli wheels on an Avanti," I yell.

'He's doing so well," she yells.

"*Hurry,* it maybe snowing in Snoqualmie!" Julia shouts.

36

Drift Angels

IT'S RAINING AGAINST THE WINDOW AS WARREN OPENS HIS thermos in Frank Sid's kitchen and begins pouring a brownish liquid into Dixie cups. Julia stares over his shoulder. There are thirty people in the house. Some are already in the living room, spreading out sleeping bags or blankets. Many are in the kitchen. Some are in the long hall that separates the bedrooms. The sun has dipped behind the steep mountains. Dusk with no shadows has spread across the Strait of Juan de Fuca toward Victoria. Lights go on in the house in that eerie glow against things not quite dark.

Warren is meticulous about the dosage. He looks at the levels in all the Dixie cups and makes adjustments from one Dixie cup to another. He has them all touching on the counter. Julia has turned her back on him to protect him from anyone who might accidentally bump him.

"Everyone to living room," she calls out. "We bring you back one at a time."

Everyone moves toward the living room. I place my sleeping bag against a wall. Natasha immediately places her sleeping bag next to mine. Dorothy Charles places her blanket next to Natasha. I sit down, open the bag and adjust the built-in pillow. I notice that there are a couple of blankets on my right. A woman I've never met soon sits on them.

"Hello," she says. "My things were here first. I hope you don't mind if I join you."

A guy across from us says, "I just got out of prison. Just kidding. I'm a prison guard. That's almost all the employment out here thanks to the spotted owl. There was a horticultural initiative for the prisoners. We let them grow a garden in the yard and this guy Sam got hold of some magic mushroom spores. All the prisoners were getting fucked up on mushrooms in prison and some of the guards too. You could see prisoners on their hands and knees picking at the garden. I tell you, prison is no place to get fucked up on magic mushrooms. It takes a lot of fortitude to function. The time I did it, I couldn't walk right and the bars were swaying. That loud clanking sound to everything, you probably wouldn't know. Everything has a clank or a bang to it. My body just shook every time I heard it. I mean *every* time. I had my buddy drive me home and I told my wife that if I ever got a chance to do some under the right environment, I might give it a try. So here I am. I know this isn't mushrooms. This person next to me is the guy Sam I was telling you about. He really did just get out of prison."

"I'm Sam," the next guy says and I realize people are introducing themselves.

I've been staring out the window. It's completely dark now out on the Strait. People are leaving the living room one-by-one and returning.

Phil McPherson says, "This is not like mushrooms. You'll be on the floor all night. Don't try to insert yourself into someone else's reality even if that person seems to need help. You all have puke bags beside you."

"Puke bags?" I hear Dorothy Charles whisper just as the girl next to me touches my shoulder because it's my turn to go into the kitchen.

Warren hands me a Dixie cup and I drink the tar.

"Horrible taste," Warren says. "Nothing like it. Tastes like it smells. That's ayahuasca."

I return to the living room and tap Natasha on the shoulder.

I am lying down with my eyes closed. I can't move. I am floating on the sea toward the rocks. There is lovely music coming from there. It's the Sirens' song. I try to take control, pull myself away from the drug, and the coils of a huge, powerful snake tighten around my chest. I let myself go and the coils ease. There's the lesson. You must have the courage to let go, to give yourself up. If you can't do that, the coils tighten. You will die. What a beautiful sound. I float toward the rocks. I experience how death will be. This is my death. I let go into the thing more powerful than I. I have to remember what death is, I say to myself. But I float not to an ending. I just float within the coils, being pulled, being pulled.

Not the girl beside me. She pukes violently. Eventually she cries out, "I want love so. Why do I fight it?"

The answer is in the question. I want to point that out to her but it's against the rules. Also she is very far away. Her puking continues at a violent rate. Soon someone else pukes. A spokesperson for the Elwa Tribe pukes. The prison guard pukes. Soon the whole room is in a puking frenzy. Someone moans with a sorrowful moan. I want to help the girl next to me. She is truly suffering. She's crying and puking and moaning. But she is so far away. I try to will myself into her space. I try to surface in her mind. All I do is enter a void. She pukes again.

Someone has put on music. It's a recording of a shaman singing. I feel hands down the front of my body but they are hands inside my body. I go with those hands. They are taking inventory. It's ayahuasca. It's the healer. The hands reach into every part of my body. I don't have a disease. I am not sick. I am physically well. I float on but not to the shore. Drift angels appear. They are translucent forms in long flowing robes. The healer identifies a point of tension in my neck. From my neck I am taken backward in my life to the moment that caused the tension. Soon the healer finds other places of pain that I carry to the grave. I am taken into the living reality of each pain. I acknowledge each scene. I've been here before when it happened and in revisits. That's the healing. I acknowledge I already know I carry each of these things. I acknowledge that each visit is to a familiar place for me, that I've been doing the work. I haven't been hiding things from myself or lying to myself. Not everything works out the way you want, but you can still love truth. You must love truth. Truth is why we're here. Someone pukes across the room. I see soldiers dressed in black marching lock step, so powerful and depressing and overwhelming and unfeeling, and I bring forward love to combat them with doubt and then with renewing strength. It's so obvious what side to be on. Why doesn't everybody get it? But we are in a test tube experiment of love versus hate.

Warren and Julia help the girl next to me into the kitchen. When did it become morning? I realize I didn't puke the whole night. Then I puke. You have to watch those self-congratulatory moments.

And when I puke I realize everyone is looking at me because it's light out and everyone is sitting up. Some are adjusting their belongings. Frank Sid is on his knees adjusting the morning fire in the woodstove.

Warren returns to the living room, sits down and says, "It's traditional to share experiences."

There are many people and talk takes time. But it's like brushing your teeth. You don't know it's going on until it's almost done. There are common experiences and differences. Drift angels are described. Snake coils are described. The prison guard cries and can't get to sharing. Julia sits the girl down next to me and she smiles but does not speak. Someone else whispers to her, "Oh, that's such a nice scarf you're wearing."

Dorothy Charles says, "I was given a magic wand from the healer," and she holds up her hand but there's nothing in it.

I turn to Natasha and she's staring at me.

"I say nothing," she says softly, gets up and runs from the living room.

I get up wobbly, trying to find my legs, and I follow her. She's standing by the kitchen door and staring out through the screen.

"I saw the one Warren calls Swims with Horses," she says, looking through the screen. "She holds a sword with both hands and kills any woman gets close to you. She never leave you. That why I leave you!" and she pushes through the screen and runs across the front yard into the morning mist. Now she's ahead of me running down the road toward the beach and I'm gaining on her as she reaches the beach. She runs toward the water. I'm running past the dying blackberries and the bare alders toward the rivulets and driftwood piles.

"Natasha," I call out and the air is choking. The fiberglass is melting. I keep pushing on the door, pushing on the door, pushing on the door. She's leaning over the fountain at Torrey Pines to take a drink. I nudge her with my hips. Her face in profile turns up from the fountain and she's so beautiful I gulp. Then I ask, "Swims with Horses, will you marry me?" and in a voice so soft, so precise and so full of self-satisfaction, she says, "I *knew* you'd ask." And I'm pushing on the door and pushing on the door and the fumes are inside my lungs. I reach for Natasha's shoulder to turn her, feel her shoulder begin to turn and what is it? Robert Frost, that thing? What? I know. "It can never lose its sense of meaning that once unfolded by surprise as it went." But I don't turn her. I run past her and I'm running, just running, running toward the seamount and the circling eagle, and crunching down on the slippery kelp bulbs where the sand turns to concrete at the ocean's edge, just running and running along that concrete, and now she's running with me, laughing and smiling, because movement. Movement is good.

THE END

Made in the USA
Charleston, SC
19 July 2012